By the Grand Canal

William Rivière

By the Grand Canal

GROVE PRESS
New York

First published in Great Britain in 2004 by Hodder and Stoughton
A division of Hodder Headline, London

This edition is printed by special arrangement with
Hodder Headline

Extract from *Under Ben Bulben* by W. B. Yeats reproduced
with the permission of A. P. Watt Ltd. on behalf of Michael B. Yeats

Printed in the United States of America

FIRST AMERICAN EDITION

Library of Congress Cataloging-in-Publication Data

Rivière, William.
  By the Grand Canal / William Rivière.
    p. cm.
  ISBN 0-8021-1793-7
  1. World War, 1939–1945—Peace—Ficiton. 2. British—Italy—Fiction.
  3. Venice (Italy)—Fiction. 4. Divorced men—Fiction. 5. Friendship—Fiction.
  6. Diplomats—Fiction. I. Title.
  PR6068.I97B9 2005
  823'.914—dc22   2004042393

Grove Press
an imprint of Grove/Atlantic, Inc.
841 Broadway
New York, NY 10003

05 06 07 08 09   10 9 8 7 6 5 4 3 2 1

Though grave-diggers' toil is long,
Sharp their spades, their muscles strong,
They but thrust their buried men
Back in the human mind again.

W.B. Yeats

I

The diplomat Hugh Thurne arrived back in Venice two days after the Armistice. It was already dusk, but as he followed the porter who was trundling a barrow with his suitcases down to the quay, he glanced around delightedly at the grey houses, dull water, brown light.

Far off, a scrawl of lightning flickered, and after several seconds faint thunder growled. A few heavy drops of rain fell, and then nothing.

Thurne was so tall, and when no action was required of him would stand so upright and so still for so long, that when he'd been at Cambridge in the nineties one young lady whom he had often taken out on the river had called him the heron, or her darling heron. Among his friends, the name had stuck. And now, immediately feeling reinvigorated to be back on the Grand Canal after the train journey from Rome, in his tweed ulster and his trilby he stood straight and immobile for a minute in the gondola, his eyes rejoicing in the vessels at the wharf. Then he sat down, crossed his long legs

1

comfortably, and at once took pleasure in a damp gust that swept the fresh-water smell of coming rain across the briny smell of the lagoon; in a stevedore who hunkered down tiredly on a bollard and squinted at the sky; in the lilting motion of the boat as the oarsman pushed off and began to row.

Practically the entire length of the Grand Canal lay before him (his house, Ca' Zante, was beyond the Accademia), and now in the chill gloom of the November nightfall the tideway winding ahead down its enfilade of facades seemed to offer all the beguilements his spirit longed for. Yes, here his disconsolate moods would hold off as they had in the past, he let himself believe, snugging his scarf more warmly around his neck, and gazing ahead down to the palaces where a few lights were beginning to shine.

Away from England, which these days was redolent of friends who'd been killed. Above all away from London, and his charade of a marriage, his charade of a family life.

When, a few years before the war, Hugh Thurne had first been beguiled by Venice, he'd been in a state of depression caused by his realisation that not only was he not in love with his wife Elizabeth but he could hardly endure to be in the same room and hear her talk. He had started to make friends in the city on the lagoon: Venetians, Americans, people from half the countries of Europe. He had made his London friends smile at the amount of time he contrived to while away at Ca' Zante, enjoying himself, they never doubted, with one enchantress after another, and generally living it up, and probably drinking rather too much. And slowly, as Hugh had hoped, he'd begun to cheer up.

2

That long-ago glorious capital of a trading empire, now reduced to a cosmopolitan, decaying village, became for him a place where he might outlive his failure as a husband. After years of spiritual stagnancy, it became a place of promise, of possible renewal. It was where, occasionally when he was with others, occasionally when he was on his own, from the deep source of his consciousness welled up moments of freedom and delight, so that – in anxious hope, but also already in dismay that this might be nothing but an *ignis fatuus* of his mind – he knew he was coming to life again.

Then the war came. For three years Thurne never set foot in Italy. But late in '17 he was on Lloyd George's staff at the Allies' conference at Rapallo, when every day brought news of the revolution in Russia and when the Italians, defeated on the Isonzo and at Caporetto, were falling back. He travelled on to Venice (where his house, which he had taken for pleasure, abruptly became a useful headquarters) ahead of the eight French and British divisions sent to the Venetian hinterland to help shore up the new defensive line along the river Piave, when one more defeat would have knocked Italy out of the war for good.

Here on his left hand loomed the church of San Marcuola, massive and lightless – no, he saw, someone was opening the door, a chink of lamplight showed and was gone. Children skirmishing on the water-steps in the gloaming, a gnarled and now leafless wisteria pergola over a jetty, a boatman's shout – wonderful! Soon he'd be drawing abreast of the Venier family house, so beautiful, so in need of repairs, so well loved by all that family – and it was dear to him too, on account of happy evenings over the years, and particularly on account of evenings last winter when, with the front line only a few miles north of the lagoon, you heard the bombardments when they started up. That time when a Hungarian division had crossed the Piave delta, which was a good deal less than twenty miles away, he'd been at dinner with Giacomo and Valentina Venier. They'd promised him, over the fish soup, that if their city fell to the Emperor of Austria's armies again, as it had in 1848, he wasn't to worry; for them to have one of His Britannic Majesty's envoys to hide in their attic till the war was over would be nothing but a pleasure.

Well, praise God they'd held the line at the river, he thought buoyantly, revelling in the soft slap and lap of the water against his black hull, in the creak of the long oar, and even finding in the gulls' desolate cries a note in harmony with his contentment to be back. That night when four German battalions had fought their way across at Ponte di Piave, but the Italian counter-attack had driven them back, and then for a change it was the defenders of their native land who were rounding up prisoners. What was more, if the line *had* been broken again, and if for some reason he hadn't been able to get away southward, it would have been delightful to roost in Giacomo and Valentina's attic and be cosseted by them.

Yes, but was he the only man who suspected that this war might turn out to have been a Pyrrhic victory? (As he always did when he was cheerful, Thurne started wondering vigorously.) Had the war been a successful exercise in standing your ground but an unsustainable injury too? What were the consequences of this long Armegeddon going to be, for Italy, for France, and above all for those British Isles where he'd happened to be bred and which therefore he happened to love? Was anybody except him afraid that the last and greatest of the maritime empires, run from an off-lying island with all the demographic and industrial weakness that entailed, might not be going to hold her own indefinitely against continental powers like America and Russia and Germany, even if the ruin of the last two of these gave the British a respite now? – and it would only be a respite. (These were exactly the sort of speculations which, emerging in recent conversations at the embassy in Rome, had caused the ambassador to grin, and to tell him that, honestly, he was far too melancholy a fellow to be let loose to represent the country overseas.) For that matter, this winter when the fighting men started to come home and be met by hollering crowds, when the job was left to special envoys such as himself, were he and his like going to be Machiavellian enough to devise peace treaties that would be effective? Were they going to be resolute enough to enforce them for years and for decades? *Was* the war over, or was this just a lull? How long would it be before the victorious alliance showed a few fissures?

Well, he wouldn't sit brooding at home this evening, he'd go and find out what old Giacomo Venier thought about the victory or thought about the mess the continent was in. He'd go to his own house now, he'd dump his kit, he'd have a wash and a drink. Then he'd find out if Valentina and Giacomo felt like inviting him to dinner or whether they'd rather he invited them.

Looking up at the Venier house as he passed it, he saw a high window suddenly bloom with light, and a girl – it must be Gloria, the daughter – stand to gaze out at the dusk and the palaces and the boats. He waved, but she hadn't seen him, or it was so nearly dark that she hadn't recognised him.

Naturally those immensely respectable Veniers would never know anything of the other delights this city held for him, Hugh mused, and smiled as his boat bore him on. No hint that, after the day-long expeditions with them on the lagoon and the merry family dinners, he might have himself rowed on elsewhere before going home. No stories of courtesans for the Veniers, heavens no. What was it that procuring wretch Tiziana Zuccarelli had murmured to him the last time they'd seen each other? 'I want you to meet my sister Emanuela, who's just starting to sing some small parts at the Fenice. She's a real Tiepolo beauty, just your type.' Something like that.

As he swayed slowly on down the darkening waterway towards Rialto, his voluptuous mind filled with a chamber (a composite of a number he had known) where brocades shrouded a bed, the air was scented with pot-pourri, and before a gilt looking-glass a young woman with Tiepolo skin and hair and eyes was beginning to take off her clothes.

The sky over the Grand Canal cracked with brilliance, thunder crashed.

The schoolgirl at her bedroom window, Gloria Venier, caught her breath. 'Come and look!' she cried to her mother, who was behind her in the room, tidying away the ironed clothes that she herself ought to have been putting into the chest-of-drawers. 'I've never seen such lightning, Mamma! Look, there it is again! It's silver-pink, and it's silver-violet, and . . .'

II

'Oh, the terms of the Armistice on the Western Front are all right.'

Speaking in Italian because, for years of peace and then of war, that had been the language of his friendship with this family, Thurne frowned cheerfully down the length of the *sala* of the Venier house, where the Murano chandelier shimmered inadequately above marquetry cabinets and carved ebony page-boys, and half the paintings were so far from the nearest lamp that only eyes familiar with them by daylight could make out what the compositions were. At the dining-table Giacomo and he had begun to tease out one another's thoughts about the victory and the peace, and now the cold, tenebrous drawing-room was suffused with how delighted they were to see each other and to have time to talk.

The storm that had battened on Venice all evening still showed no inclination to move away across the lagoon. Standing beside his host at the tall windows over the Grand Canal, which were trembling in their infirm frames as if they had St Vitus's dance, Hugh broke off for a peal of thunder directly overhead.

'Heavens, I hope your chimneys are all right! Yes, if anyone thinks we're being too harsh, they ought to remember the terms the Germans imposed on the French forty-whatever years ago after their last war. For that matter, they could try to explain how we can stop Germany being her old self again in a few years *except* by putting her army and navy out of action, or how in France they can feel half-way safe *unless* their troops and ours move forward to the Rhine and hold bridgeheads over it. No, that's not the problem. Oh I say, Giacomo, thank you. What wonderful firewater is this?' He raised his glass to his nose. 'Calvados!'

Giacomo Venier gave the decanter a gloomy, critical stare, and said gruffly, 'Well, it ought not to taste too bad. But what is the real problem, in your view? The Austro-Hungarian empire is finished!' His voice suddenly grating with pride, he straightened his back till he was nearly standing to attention.

Hugh chuckled at this dour rejoicing in the destruction of Venice's ancestral enemy. 'The potential problem is that damned Kaiser Bill's forces are surrendering to us in Belgium and in France, when possibly we should have taken the trouble to hound them out of there and finish them off, don't you think? Another fortnight, perhaps as little as another week, would have been enough to turn a defeat into a rout. All that's happened back in Germany so far is that they've heard they've lost some battles on the Western Front, the scale of this naturally being played down by their newspapers, and now they've heard that their lousy cabinet ministers and

field marshals have rather rapidly acknowledged themselves
beaten, by this expedient inducing us to agree to negotiate,
or rather, because we've had no need to negotiate, inducing
us to state our terms.'

Venier had been born only a few years before Thurne, but
since his heart-attack he'd been an old, dying man; his moustache, his whiskers and the bristle on his bony head were
white. Listening attentively, and giving a boisterous scowl
when a clap of thunder made him miss a few words, he
lumbered half-way back down the *sala* to the fireplace and
lowered himself into an armchair.

'Of course, Giacomo, *we* know that the Kaiser's top brass
have only caved in because they've been admirably frightened by the insurrections and the mutinies that, with any
luck, are bringing their regime down.' Sauntering after his
host down the long room, Hugh Thurne spoke in the confident, quiet voice of a man accustomed to having mastered
his brief, to having thought out what he wanted to say, and
to knowing how to say it; but he kept glancing at Giacomo
Venier with affectionate, quizzical eyes to find out what
response his ideas were getting. 'But in German towns and
villages what impressions will they have received? I reckon
it might have been better if they'd actually *seen* their divisions reduced to a rabble that we and our allies were herding
up. We don't want our sons who are schoolboys now, or the
sons that any of us may have in the next few years, to have
to fight this war all over again as soon as they're men. Oh
Lord, how unconvinced I can get! And just when everyone
else has been hurling their hats in the air, and letting off

fireworks, and getting drunk. Certainly most people's straightforward longing for the shooting to stop as soon as possible is a lot more attractive than my apprehensions. But you've heard what the French High Command are already muttering? – that this peace is only a ceasefire for twenty years.'

Hugh stooped and put another log on the fire. Away in the shadows at the Grand Canal end of the room, the long curtains trembled in the draught.

Giacomo Venier did not reply at once. In his old-fashioned coat and trousers, which he'd inherited from his father, who also in his fifties had grown flabby and contemplative, with a heave he tried to get more comfortable in his chair.

God damn it, he was thinking, Hugh's hair was thinning a bit but not much, and grizzling a bit but not much – was the fellow never going to deteriorate? The same interminable legs as ever, particularly noticeable when he stood up straight by the chimneypiece and brushed the wood dust off his hands and lit a cheroot. The same blue eyes musing behind his gold-rimmed spectacles; the same gold watch-chain looped between his waistcoat pockets, presumably only in order to draw attention to how his stomach was still concave not convex . . . Yes, and no doubt he was still the same wandering, international consolation for young ladies languishing in stagnant marriages.

What the master of the house said after a minute's brooding was: 'You've been down in Rome. What's it like in our ministries right now? Pretty disgusting, eh?'

'Well . . .' Hugh had been enjoying the cheerful lamps

dotted about the *sala*, and the purely symbolic illumination offered by the chandelier. Allowing himself to exclaim irrelevantly, 'Dear God, it's good to be here again!', he brought his attention back.

'I mean,' Giacomo pursued, 'I remember you talking last winter about how after Caporetto the consternation in our government was pretty unedifying. I imagine that this month those self-same political grandees and military grandees can't open their mouths without being revoltingly triumphant.'

Hugh shrugged. 'I've been going out to tramp the streets on my own for an hour or two before dinner. It clears all the deviousness and the pomposity out of my head, and I get some exercise, and I think of other things. I've always liked Rome in winter.'

'That's not difficult!' His brown eyes twinkling, Giacomo harrumphed with satisfaction as he decided that this was the moment for his attack. 'And you're here now because . . .' He took a sip of his Calvados, to prolong for a few more delicious seconds the pleasure of anticipation. 'Well, I'll tell you why we have the honour of your company this evening, my dear fellow. It's because after you've had your walk along the Tiber in the twilight, and after you've poked your head into a favourite church maybe, you return to your embassy, do you not? – where over dinner you talk about what to do next. Because England and France aren't going to let this wretched Italy enforce her own future frontiers with what's left of Austria-Hungary, are they? What gets fixed upon for my country at the Peace Conference some time next year, whether or not I'm still alive to grumble about it, will be what the

Americans and the two remaining Great Powers on this side of the Atlantic decide. And this new balance of the European states – some of them brand-new states, it already looks like, invented states that may turn out splendidly but may not . . . Well, it'll be what on paper looks commendably liberal and advanced, and what in fact will be simplicity itself for you to dominate.'

'Let's hope we remember to keep dominating. But that's not the immediate point.'

Hugh Thurne was still feeling inspirited to be back in this household where he'd found affection and robust spirits when his own life had lacked both those. But he knew that his old friend enjoyed being pugnacious on occasion just as much as at other times he liked being apparently inconsequential, so he smiled and took up the tussle.

'For a start, Giacomo, Rome's position is nothing like as strong as we might wish it to be. This nation's capacity to go on making war effectively is very near indeed to being as finished as Austria's, and civil society here has been brought almost as close to collapse as it has there. Secondly, if you bring up that irresponsible secret treaty between your country and mine . . . For pity's sake, you know as well as I do that when there's a war on our political lords and masters will sign *anything*. But at the Peace Conference you'll get the Alto Adige, and the Trentino, and a border right up at the Brenner Pass, if you negotiate with any astuteness at all. Whether these gratifying acquisitions are worth upward of six hundred thousand men killed is a question that luckily it's not my job to pontificate about. What's going to happen to Trieste I'm not sure. As for Istria, and the Dalmatian coast, I wouldn't—'

'So you're one of the first extraneous souls to pitch up in these parts to help us start fiddling around with our frontiers,' Giacomo butted in, growling contentedly. 'Good – I've understood! That's all right! Look, the decanter is by your elbow. You could help me to another drop too. And, of course, you can't actually *get* to poor defeated Vienna right now. And if you did get there, you'd be more likely to be stabbed by a starving boy stealing your watch than to have some beribboned imperial courtier invite you to dinner in the manner that you found so agreeable whenever there were discussions to be initiated back in that lost life we had before the war. So you'll be cluttering up the dinner parties here in this lagoon of ours for a while. Excellent!' Then he demanded abruptly: 'Have you been getting depressed?'

'Of course I have!' Hugh Thurne gave a breath of laughter, and set down his glass on the mantelpiece by his shoulder. 'What do you expect? I get worse and worse! I went down with bronchitis, which didn't help, and afterward I escaped to our place near the sea to convalesce, and because, well, to have stayed cooped up in London with Elizabeth would have made me suicidal, but fortunately she hates the country. She's having an affair with a brigadier from Massachusetts, did you know? A fellow called Bill Knox. He's been seconded to their embassy in London, as a military attaché or something of that sort. I've met him a couple of times, he seems all right.'

Hugh shook his head in bewilderment, and this time he laughed aloud.

'Honestly, what a marriage! I mean – the odd life one will die having led! At any rate, as you've guessed . . . All autumn, while our army in France was winning some of the greatest victories in its history, this contemptible specimen of manhood was . . . Dear God, days came when I could scarcely walk down the lane to post a letter, for the misery piled up in my head. Every morning I'd set to work to coax my mind or my spirit or what-have-you into action, or at least into a sensible indifference. By evening I'd be thanking my defective lungs that I didn't need to face the Foreign Office again quite yet, at the same time as I'd be longing for some work to lose myself in. And then, after a couple of months . . . Heavens, if only one understood these things!'

Hugh flopped down onto a chaise-longue, joined his hands as if in prayer, rested his chin on his finger-tips, and turned to his host as if he truly expected that if, for a few instants, he contemplated those smiling, caustic eyes, those creased jowls, and that pale lump of skull with its well-brushed white tussocks, the miasma in his own head would be dispelled.

'You know, it's really very strange, how one is invariably rescued, or how I've hitherto been rescued – though one can't but be aware that the year may come when one's melancholy doesn't lift. But thanks to Lord knows what physiological or psychological rhythms . . . At all events, the merciful time comes when I can *feel* my wits becoming more ironical, more amused.'

'And what was it that you were thinking about gloomily then and you're thinking about more sanguinely now? Oh hello, darling.' Slower than Hugh, who had seen Valentina first, Giacomo hauled himself to his feet. 'Come and sit by the fire. We've been commandeering the only few square metres in the house that are even remotely warm.'

III

Valentina Venier was just as fond of Hugh Thurne as her husband was, but her liking for him was a lot more complicated. Each time he cropped up in Venice, old doubts and distresses would niggle at her, until the pleasure of seeing him again had its assuaging but also dulling effect, and she went back to trying to forget certain things and not make too much of others.

Valentina was worldly enough to have decided long ago that, since poor Hugh's marriage had manifestly been a flop, the only thing to do was to smile at his liaisons, which at least had the great merit of being nothing if not superficial. What tormented her, the minute she saw that elegant, elongated man striding along the alley toward the street door of her house, or disembarking at her canal gate, was the thought of how wretched he must be to be so estranged from his two sons, who were at a prep school in Oxfordshire, and then the worse thought that he was not so downcast as all that. After which it would be hopeless, the whole hornets' nest of her disquiets would start buzzing in her head.

The long struggle to give Francesco and Gloria at least approximately the sort of upbringing she believed in, and the attempt to look after the ramshackle palace her husband had inherited (unfortunately without inheriting the family fortune, which before it was dissipated had made the lives of previous ladies of the house a lot easier), had left her anxious, dumpy, played out, with her wispy hair going grey, whereas Hugh, who was the same age, looked years younger. Valentina had learned to be merely amused by this. Even so, she couldn't rid herself of the suspicion that one reason Hugh remained so debonair was that he'd never let his private life become anything other than a succession of transient pleasures, or let himself be borne down by any responsibility that couldn't be shifted by the writing of a cheque. And it was all very fine, the way he'd breeze in to partake of Giacomo's and her family life for a day or for an evening, always brimming with his delight to be back here and brimming with praise for the children – and she was glad if in this household of hers they succeeded in offering him some sort of sanctuary, or love, or spiritual sustenance that he needed. But didn't he realise that, like a lot of people whose marriages had become simulacra, he was just rather easily idealising what others with more perseverance, and perhaps with greater humility or greater magnanimity, had most imperfectly achieved? Could he really contrive not to know that even in the happiest families the merriment was often distinctly intermittent and the love problematic?

Tonight Valentina had been dogged by her recurrent fear (which neither her husband nor Hugh Thurne had ever suspected in her for an instant) that the friendship between the two men was not as equal as it ought to be. It should have been perfectly obvious, from the atmosphere in the house this evening, as on dozens of previous evenings, that her fear was groundless. But the habits of lack of self-confidence and of anxious wondering were so engrained in Valentina that her distress had generated its own momentum and was taking several hours to die away.

Hugh came from a family of undistinguished gentry, failing farmers; but his career in the diplomatic service had been relentlessly in the ascendant, he'd married a millionairess, last year he'd been knighted, he had cabinet ministers as well as ambassadors among his backers. Giacomo had attempted to revive his family's condition a little. He'd become a lawyer with a practice near Rialto bridge. For many years he'd worked conscientiously though not ruthlessly, so that now, as he would announce wryly, the decline of the Veniers had been brought under a modicum of control and was proceeding in a more orderly fashion. But did Hugh really look forward to their meetings as keenly as she knew her husband did? Ever since Giacomo had been ill, he'd gone nowhere, he'd lived in such a small way – and Venice was so provincial!

When Valentina came into the *sala* she had nearly finished worrying and was nervously exhausted. She sat down, as encouraged to, close enough to the hearth for the firelight to play its glimmer on her black silk dress, which she wore with an amethyst brooch on the ruffle at her throat.

She said: 'Francesco has gone out to the café to play billiards with some of his university friends. And Gloria says she's going to bed, which means she's curled up with some romantic novel or other.' Then she gave the two men a tired, vague, expectant smile.

Hugh Thurne knew how Valentina fretted about her family; he had often tried to encourage her, and to offer advice and help; but he was blithely unaware that he himself had ever been the cause of her tense brooding. He drifted back to the windows and drew aside a curtain. The thunder was far off now, but one of the last flarings in the sky lit up the houses on the other side of the Grand Canal, and the church of San Stae, and the cascades of rain.

'What have I been thinking?' he echoed Giacomo's last question, his ideas about the war and the victory still tumbling over one another in his head. 'Well, I'll tell you a few questions that have been bedevilling me,' he began readily, in a voice that did not sound remotely bedevilled.

'One thing is that . . . Naturally to have been defeated would have been immeasurably worse, so from a political point of view you can say that our torments and our crimes in this war have been less utterly in vain than those of our enemies. But am I the only dejected idiot who can't help pointing out to himself that – irrespective of this alliance or that alliance ending up brandishing flags and shouting hurrah – an immense evil has been done, which can certainly never be undone or atoned for? And what's it going to be like the next time we all go to war, since our means of slaughtering each other seem bound to go on getting more mechanised and efficient? Ah, you'll say, but we've learned, here in the Old World. This time we've horrified ourselves good and proper. We shan't go to war against one another again. And even if we're not capable of learning, there's that nice fellow from the New World, there's that rather high-minded President Wilson, who's already started ticking us off and laying down rules for how we must behave from now on. But – if the less barbarous, when all else has been tried and has failed, have no other means than war of defending themselves against the more barbarous?

'Here's a further thought that arises from that. The Americans came into the war toward the end, their whole society won't have been vitiated by these years. But here on our side of the ocean, where the butcher's bill, when finally it gets totted up at least roughly right, is going to come to – what? – well, a lot more than five million men killed in action, but with any luck not double that. I won't speak of the dead. But the bereft . . . It's not easy to conceive of grief and despair on this scale, or imagine what effects this ruining of lives right across a continent is going to have, what the abstract reverberations of the war will be. Are we going to be good at taking decisions that are brave, humane, far-sighted?

'Or look at it from the political point of view. Between us we seem to have managed the destruction of four empires. Here in the West our democracy and our liberal society have all the defects we like to point out to each other. But in most of the lands that formed the German and the Russian empires, and in the lands that till last week were Austro-Hungarian dominions and Ottoman dominions, their traditions are of despotism and militarism. Are the survivors really going to put better systems in place, and nurture what we think of as enlightened traditions so the new systems thrive instead of failing?

'Now lastly – and then I'll shut up about this. Here in this country, and in France, and in my country, we've at least defended ourselves. We've stayed on our feet, just. And to be in the winning alliance feels pretty good. There's no particular risk of military coups in our capital cities this month, our national currencies are still worth something, food and medical supplies are still getting through. Here the three of us lounge by your fire – and you've got enough logs to keep you going all through the winter, haven't you? – unlike a lot of people in towns north of here where they used to be bossed around by the Hapsburgs or the Hohenzollerns or the Romanovs. What taxes me isn't whether or not I can hear political gangs or marauders shooting in the alley behind the house, but whether to light another of these excellent cheroots now or in five minutes.

'But – well – tell me what you think of this. Our failures when they arrive, or when they become unmistakable, may be quite different from defeat in war. They may have nothing to do with the brisk, adroit altering of national constitutions (which if you'd happened to win the war you wouldn't have altered) and the convenient forgetting of quite large empires. Take Britain, which I reckon is in a far worse condition than we've yet realised. Our downfall may easily consist in the winning of European wars so catastrophic they leave us nervously enfeebled, half-way to bankruptcy, stuffed to the eyeballs with self-congratulation, and as weak as a litter of kittens. Whereas the only strategy for an island as small as ours, if we feel like staying in the business of being a Great Power, is going to have to be . . .' He grinned. 'Hell, I'll tell you when I've worked it out.'

'Oh, you English will go the way that we Venetians went.' Giacomo's white hedges of eyebrows rose and fell above his imperturbable, coruscating, contented stare. 'I know that your home island is God knows how many times our cluster of muddy shoals in this lagoon and the mainland provinces we used to have – but even so, the logic is the same, and it's inexorable.'

Self-contained and motionless in his charcoal-grey suit, all the while the man whose friends called him a heron had been speaking he'd stood as if the drawing-room had been an opaque pond with a few eddies of light, and he had been that gaunt fisher, perfectly vertical and changeless over the sedge on the bank, watching, waiting. But now Hugh had remembered one death among all the deaths. He raised his finger-tips to his forehead and rubbed. He looked around wearily for an armchair; he sat down.

'Thinking of England, and thinking of Philip being killed . . . When I wrote to Violet, I invited her out here, and now the war is over and people can travel again I expect she'll come before too long. There's the whole top floor of Ca' Zante, where nobody ever goes. I could have it tidied up for her. And for Robert too, of course, in his school holidays. In a while, when she feels up to it, for her to get completely away from her previous life might be a good idea, don't you feel? You know she's going to lose that lovely old house, and the woods and the meadows, everything. It'll go to Philip's son by his first marriage.'

Jolted into recalling Philip Mancroft's death, Valentina had given a gasp of distress. She was looking away into the gloom, her lips pressed tightly together.

Because he knew what his wife was about to say, and in order to give her time to collect herself, Giacomo said gruffly: 'That poor lad, Robert . . . He must be in his last year at Eton by now, I suppose. It's just as frightful for him as for his mother. To be summoned to some ghastly study, and told that his father has been killed. And to lose the house where he was brought up, to lose all his childhood . . . His christening was the first time that you and I met, remember?'

'I'm sorry, Hugh. You took me by surprise.' Valentina restored her handkerchief to her reticule, which had silk tassels from which dangled tiny jet elephants and lions. 'My darling Violet, I can't bear it for her! I've been so fortunate, but she! Another few weeks and it would all have been over, and eventually he would have come home. And Mesopotamia seems such a long way off to be killed, and not much to do with us here. Oh dear, that's not a very military remark, is it? It was in a cavalry attack, we were told – is that true, do you know? If so, that's just like Philip. No, but what I wanted to say was, when Giacomo and I wrote to Violet we too invited her here. And she's already written back. She's coming to stay with us in the spring.'

IV

The rain had blown over. When Hugh started off between the tall, dank houses to walk back to Ca' Zante, the cloudy night smelled of puddles.

The dead young soldiers of Venice were all about him, as he walked beside the canals where they'd rowed their skiffs, as his footfalls sounded in the porticoes where they'd kissed their girls. Those who would never recover from those deaths were all about him too. He sensed them above him behind shuttered windows as he crossed a bridge or turned into an alley. They were there: sitting up late by a lamp or lying on their beds, their eyes glistening, remembering a son, a brother, a father, a husband, a sweetheart. But in Hugh's grimly sanguine mood tonight, what struck him was how quickly the shrieks of men dying on battlefields, and the shrieks of women when the news came, ceased to be heard, and how they'd have almost no effect on the generations who lived afterward. The spirits of the lost men who'd been boys in this labyrinth of ditches and façades still seemed to linger beneath an archway, by a mooring, in a courtyard, if you had a mind's eye and a mind's ear for such hauntings – but they wouldn't for long. Grief would dull as the years passed; then as the decades passed the grievers would die; it would all be over.

The shadowy branches of a fig tree over a garden wall, the last of its leathery leaves blown by a gust past a street-lamp and sent rasping wetly away over the flagstones – tonight all things seemed good to Hugh. It had been cold in the Venier drawing-room even if you kept close to the fire, but now he felt warm and invigorated, striding along baled in his tweed ulster; and just as it had been excellent to see his old friends for a few hours, now it was excellent to be on his own again. He wondered if Francesco's parents truly supposed that his undergraduate friends and he dedicated their evenings exclusively to the billiard table. He imagined fifteen-year-old Gloria propped up on her elbow in bed, her bunchy black hair falling forward as she read – what? who would her favourite story-tellers be?

Giacomo Venier was a patrician without a state to be a patrician of, that was his problem, Hugh suddenly decided and smiled, along with the old fellow's other problem of never having any money to speak of in his bank account. Typical, too, how he couldn't contemplate any half-way func-tioning civilisation, the English for instance, without predicting with saturnine satisfaction that it would go the way his had gone.

But if Giacomo was right? For that matter, if he himself, and Joe Chamberlain, and a dozen other men he'd talked to about this were right in their forebodings? If the United Kingdom had indeed been in economic decline and consequently in international political decline for a generation at least, so that out-fighting their enemy empires in this war, though a stupendous achievement, wasn't going to answer the fundamental question . . .? Would people in England look back afterward, as they'd been doing here in Venice for upward of a hundred years, and hold forth to each other sanctimoniously about quite how tawdry the splendour had been toward the end, how inwardly corroded the power had been, how illusory the superiority, and what a despicable crew the so-called elite had been?

The elite . . . Lucky fellows like Philip Mancroft who'd inherited Brack Hall, and a couple of months ago had been campaigning with his yeomanry regiment somewhere between the Tigris and the Euphrates when he'd had a bullet plugged into him by some honest Turkish rifleman trying to defend himself against attack. Then others, who hadn't inherited anything much, the climbers like he himself who'd . . . (Hugh had reached the low iron bridge at the Accademia. With a quick impulse of hope, he glanced left down the Grand Canal to pick out Ca' Zante in the murky night, to hold up before his spirit for a moment the promise of freedom and renewal that house held for him.) Well, he'd decided by the time Philip and he were at Cambridge that he wasn't going to live in the poky, provincial way his parents had lived, that things would be more amusing nearish to the top. So he'd got himself a reputation for – oh – for ability, in some quarters, and for ambition and ruthlessness in other quarters. Then rather more likeable climbers like Violet, who hadn't been twenty before she'd jumped into bed with the fine things of this world, and now stood to lose a good few of them. No, that wasn't fair; or at least, it wasn't that simple.

Hugh smiled as he tramped, remembering how dowdily horrified Violet's parents had been to envisage their harum-scarum daughter somehow contriving to meet the scandalously divorced landowner and young Liberal grandee Philip Mancroft, and then how, practically the next week, they'd been incredulous with delight and pride when it transpired that he had every intention of making her the chatelaine of Brack Hall, if she would consent to meet him at Chelsea Register Office one morning. And for heaven's sake – the old dears had been right to be astonished! He himself, each and every one of the man's friends – they'd all imagined that, once Violet had with some panache magicked herself into a girl who was invited to Brack and to a few other establishments in the county comparable to it, Philip would content himself with her delightful readiness, after a dance, to find herself in his bedroom. His first marriage had been horrible; he was in the habit of having lovers. And now, when after – what? – oh, after eighteen-odd years, during which Violet in many ways hadn't changed a bit. When now she was the same lovely chestnut-headed ragamuffin as ever, only rather a classy ragamuffin on account of plenty of Mancroft veneer having been applied to her, and this autumn suddenly she was on her own. Without Philip to bring them together, or for that matter without Philip to keep them apart, were Violet and he going to find it straightforward to continue their old teasing, affectionate camaraderie? Well, they were going to *have* to get back into the swing of it.

Hugh hoicked his key out of his coat pocket, standing at the street door to his house, where at the foot of the alley the Grand Canal whispered.

How chancy everything was! and how topsy-turvy! Philip and he had rowed in the same Trinity eight, they were each godfather to one of the other's sons, for a quarter of a century they'd met at dinner parties, they'd gone to race meetings together – but already he was almost accustomed to Philip not being there any more, to Philip being in the past. Just think, if it had been the other way around. If it had been he who'd come to grief. If it had been Philip who, one night at the beginning of the new peace, had found himself at the door of a house in Italy that he'd rented, had found himself remembering, and wondering, and no doubt hoping that the years to come might bring him flickers of happiness of one sort or another. Much better that way around, of course. Instead of Violet with her passionate heart having her delight in life scrumpled up and tossed into the waste-paper basket, Elizabeth could have waited for a discreet year or two and then married her brigadier.

Ca' Zante and its contents had been bought and sold a number of times, twice even in the last hundred years; rooms had been redecorated, refurnished. The late fifteenth-century shell was magnificent, with its bas-reliefs on the marble stair-case and on the round-headed arches. But it was only a shell. It wasn't redolent of anyone's past, which was why at this juncture of his life Hugh Thurne liked it.

Haunted tonight by the entwinings of other people's destinies with his own, haunted by mirrorings, by ironies, the instant he stepped into the colonnaded hall with its Corinthian capitals he recalled the last time he'd seen Violet Mancroft and her son, in the summer. He'd been down at his place near the North Sea for a few days, so he'd driven over to Brack, where in Philip's absence she'd been overseeing the harvest enthusiastically day after day from sunrise till dusk. She'd shown him the latest letter that had reached her from Mesopotamia, which Philip said the troopers sensibly called Mess-pot. The three of them had eaten lunch – gammon, potatoes, a glass of beer – with the dining-room windows open, so that they could hear the wood-pigeons, and then they'd hurried back to the fields being reaped. Whereas now . . . Wherever she was lingering tonight, in that house where all the furniture and the paintings, all the china and the silver, everything had come down from Philip's parents and his grandparents, in that house where her husband had been a child and her son had been a child – wherever in those sad rooms she was standing or sitting, she was saying goodbye, she was getting ready to go away and never come back.

Hugh took off his trilby, loosened his scarf and started to take off his ulster, but then he huddled it back on and began to pace up and down the length of the pillared hall. These lanterns burning, one by the canal gate and one near the foot of the staircase and the archway into the garden; this marble well-head where people always seemed to dump their hats and umbrellas; the fireplace of different marbles, Veronese red, green, grey . . . All this impersonal loveliness, which in degraded Venice you could rent for a few years if the fancy took you, was the sort of exile and solitude, was the sort of shiftless cosmopolitan liberty that he'd grasped at because it might offer some glimmer of salvation, whereas poor Violet was being evicted into it. And all this driftwood left bobbing about after the war, the soldiers and sailors when they came home, the widows like Violet, the fellows like himself who'd been in cushy jobs, people like the Veniers who couldn't conceivably have been of use to any nation's war effort – how were they really going to react? And what was it that he ought to have been able to say to Valentina and Giacomo this evening, but hadn't because his imagination hadn't yet done the work?

Well, he thought, robustly enough to surprise himself with a twinge of intellectual pleasure, it wasn't so difficult as all that to start to get to grips with. Those whose nature it was to be self-righteous and to busy themselves with other people's affairs would decide that, thanks to all this slaughtering, they had mysteriously become more enlightened than their fore-bears, and now might construct a more presentable society. Others with different natures would fritter their remaining years away trying to dream the past back to life. But if you couldn't quite bring yourself to be gulled in either of those ways, what awaited you?

That was too difficult for the time being, so Hugh's mind veered off in more practical directions. Rejoicing in the thought of the whole empty, silent palace above his head, where the housekeeper before she went home would have left a lamp shining in this room and that to welcome him, he sauntered up and down the hall more idly now, his scarf swinging, his overcoat unbuttoned, his hands in his trouser pockets, pausing, glancing.

Supposing he *didn't* get the Rome embassy when the present chap's time there was up – what then? He knew that in Whitehall and also in Downing Street he'd been mentioned as a strong candidate, even as a very nearly obvious choice. On the other hand, some of his superiors in the service couldn't stand his guts, a sentiment they masked by being of the opinion that he was 'a brilliant man in his line' who, doubtless, would always be useful as an expert behind the scenes, but 'not quite the right stuff, you know. A question of character. It always comes out, in the end.'

By the same token, his knighthood might perfectly reasonably be seen as a sign of approval from on high. Equally, it might turn out to be what he was given instead of one of the great ambassadorships.

Well, what about that other dream he'd cherished in indolent, inconsequential hours, what about chucking up the diplomatic service after twenty-five years? When he'd acknowledged failure in his family life it had been an act of desperation, it had been the only way to survive at all. But perhaps if he acknowledged that in his profession he'd reached his limit it might be a further liberation, it might be a chance to be different from now on. He could base himself here in Venice, and for half of each year he'd travel. He might even end up by writing the study of British imperial strategy for which he'd been jotting down notes for years.

But this train of thought, too, led toward the vexed question of whether it would be possible to be less unhappy in the future, questions of self-knowledge that he longed to doubt and of hopes that he longed to trust, so once more his mind recoiled. Chuckling to reflect that, if he was offered the Rome embassy, it would take him all of five seconds to decide that he'd never been remotely interested in writing any damned book, he went upstairs.

V

When Philip Mancroft at twenty-nine had precipitately married Violet, Hugh Thurne had understood instinctively that the man's romantic piracies were pretty much over; Philip's eyes and heart had found their final love for their final woman, his mind had lit upon a congeries of images that would satisfy him as nearly as one was ever satisfied. Hugh had rejoiced for his friend, and his own engagement and marriage shortly afterward had been borne forward on the cheerful conviction that he, too, who so far had stumbled along through life pretty idiotically, had suddenly, and of course through no virtue of his own, emerged into a propitious time when everything from now onward was going to be clearer and simpler, at last everything was going to ring true.

How he'd fallen heels over head for Elizabeth! What a fool of himself he'd made, shyly and happily introducing her to Philip and Violet. It had never occurred to him until the following year that they must have started practically at once to ask each other whether she could conceivably be the right girl for him.

Then for month after month, everywhere that he'd been invited for lunch or for dinner, he'd heaved the conversation around to the outstanding talents and the unostentatious merits of his fiancée's in fact exceedingly ordinary though decent family. He'd taken her brother to see *Measure for Measure*, when the simple fellow would have far preferred to be left at his club to natter about the stock exchange and to dine over-indulgently. Six weeks later, he'd compounded the error by taking him to *Troilus and Cressida*.

Even now, as in Venice at the beginning of 1919 Hugh embarked on an affair with Emanuela Zuccarelli, the memory of the year of his wedding could make him flush miserably. He was still recalling Elizabeth's nice, unimaginative father (vice-chairman of a merchant bank) with guilt and with liking. He was still rueful about how, though of course he hadn't had the honesty to confront this at the time, Elizabeth's wealth *had* been part of her glamour for him.

Emanuela's fashionably slim dresses, her cigarette-holders, her partying – to Hugh everything about her said flapper, said uncommonly pretty girl about town, and their affair began in perfect accordance with age-old, civilised understandings.

These rules of elegant conduct most peremptorily specified the following. Firstly, that attraction must be irresistible, or at least must be presented as being so, since no man or woman of spirit would wish to be seen to bother to satisfy a mild erotic curiosity or an indolent desire. Secondly, that a little flirtatious sparring before seduction was in good taste, but more than a little was a bore. Thirdly, that there must be no other extant attachments, or if, as was unfortunately often the case, regrettable encumbrances existed, owing either to romantic naïveté in the past or to social or pecuniary considerations in the present, their existence must never by a flicker of an eyelash be alluded to. Lastly that, just as no uncalled-for questions should be asked, so most categorically must no demands ever be permitted, or the affair be made less delightful by being allowed to develop any unbecoming seriousness.

Both Hugh Thurne and Emanuela Zuccarelli had lived by these sensible precepts for some years, with excellent results. This new liaison, too, had begun, like so many which run their courses without producing undue unhappiness, simply because there was no very pressing reason for not beginning it. But by early in the year they were taking headlong delight in one another, and had started consistently to mistake carnal excitement for all manner of nebulous sentiments and imaginings.

Emanuela's sister was right: she might easily have been the model for Pharoah's daughter in Giambattista Tiepolo's *The Finding of Moses*. She might have modelled for *Venus and Time* too, in which the gems in the goddess's golden hair and on her white throat appear to be the same. Ever since she'd been fifteen or so, people had told Emanuela she was a Tiepolo girl, and now when this enchanted her new lover she dressed with hints of the master's style and of his colours as often as Hugh pleased.

The war was over, the foreigners and their money were coming back to Venice, the theatres were opening to the public again, including La Fenice where she had once or twice been elevated from her worthy namelessness in the chorus to sing minor roles – Emanuela was already in high spirits and determined to enjoy herself. Fashionable life on the Lido would pick up once more when the first season of the new peace began. She would go back to feeling slightly dizzy and slightly triumphant in the Excelsior's ball-room and its dining-room, on its awninged terraces and its scrupulously raked beach, which were the only places, in her opinion, where practically everybody had gaiety and chic to match her own, though not many of the girls when they swanned through a door would instantly have all eyes upon them as she would. Hugh Thurne possessed for her a double attractiveness: he was a prestigious catch, and he scarcely impinged on her independence because he was in Venice so infrequently and could never stay for more than a few days.

After a girlhood in provincial singing schools and rehearsal rooms, at first Emanuela found her new lover almost awesomely distinguished, and wonderfully good-looking. At her last birthday she had awoken to the fact that she was closer to thirty than to twenty: light-hearted superficiality no longer seemed to her the *only* sophisticated way to behave when it came to men; semi-conscious calculations intruded themselves into her dreamings; she was ready to feel romantic, if the right chords were touched, if it seemed a good idea. Hugh Thurne's having a whole palace on the Grand Canal made going to him there thoroughly satisfactory, though it was a little disappointing that Ca' Zante was only rented. Still, no doubt such an eminent man would be able to buy himself a pleasant place, if he saw a reason to. Above all Emanuela had, to a high degree, the ability (which Hugh soon envied) to live each year and each minute as it came. So she abandoned herself to her affair joyously, and almost forgot the urbane detachment that hitherto she'd been so good at flaunting beneath chandeliers and on promenades.

As for Hugh, however dourly or mockingly he reminded himself that he'd be a lot happier if he could refrain from falling in love, soon he was imagining a future in which Emanuela would dependably be beside him, or at least, that being practically impossible, always be waiting for him when he got back to Venice. His own utterly natural constancy to her, which astonished and delighted him, bound him into the madness of needing to know that she was his and only his. He knew that all this offended against the principles which for years had ensured that his relations with young women had had, if no other merit, at least that of alleviating rather than aggravating his melancholia. But what could he do? There was the way that, when he went to fetch her from her singing teacher's house near the Greek church, if he was so much as a minute late she'd already be waiting on the quay, sometimes holding her parasol with self-conscious stylish-ness and sometimes twiddling it forgetfully, her vivid eyes searching for him. There was the way that when his gondo-lier brought her to Ca' Zante she'd hurry into the hall, calling out to the housekeeper to know where in the house he was – and then, as soon as no one else was in the room, she'd glance around gaily to make absolutely sure, she'd jump into his arms for kisses and more kisses.

Well before Easter, Hugh had lost the last traces of his ability to doubt that she was rejoicing in her love affair in the same straightforward manner that she rejoiced in her native city on spring days and on spring nights, rejoiced that she was young and the war was over.

The affair at once developed rituals, utterly extrinsic to anything the lovers might feel, but which their relations principally consisted of. These rituals were from the start an invitation not to worry about any deficiencies of the intrinsic, and on afternoons of unease were an invitation to repeat the actions which in the past had produced a pleasant confidence that things would go on like this, and pleasant concupiscence, and a pleasant haze in the brain.

One of their rituals was to visit the *couturier*, where they would choose for Emanuela silks of Tiepolo's reds and yellows and blues. Another was that they'd venture forth in the Ca' Zante boat to search out girls that Tiepolo had painted.

They'd get themselves invited to palaces; or they'd contrive to have opened, for their romantic pleasure, dilapidated public buildings – cobwebbed, streaked with damp – that were generally locked. With their necks cricked, they'd gaze up at ceilings where perhaps a blonde's superb white thigh and adorned ankle emerged from billowing silks and from cumulus, and Hugh might say: 'There you are again!'

Emanuela would smile. Standing so close beside him that he could breathe the sandalwood mingled with sea air on her skin, she'd enter into the game. 'Yes, that's me!' she might exclaim. Or, 'No, that's Emilia, the one he really liked. Heavens, what positions he'd have us pose in! Still, it does look as if the whole scene was way up in the sunlight and the clouds, doesn't it?'

VI

Emanuela Zuccarelli lived near the Madonna dell'Orto. Her rooms faced south over the tranquil quay and canal, and to Hugh they immediately summoned up wry memories of the sybarite's chamber he'd imagined on the nightfall of his November return to Venice. The ornate looking-glass (in the sixteen-hundreds style, but probably made five years ago) and the ormolu table seemed familiar. So did the lustrous brocades on the four-poster bed, and the lamps like arum lilies, and the jade oddments.

When spring came, Emanuela's green and white canvas blinds on their spindly brass rods were let down against the glorying sun all day. If the lovers raised them early in the evening, the burning core of the universe, reflected trembling ignominiously in the mucky canal, was reflected a second time on their ceiling, a bulbous growth of light quivering and asymmetrically fattening and dwindling as passing boats' ripples toyed with it.

On days when Hugh Thurne's mind was not bedevilling

him too badly, after a long afternoon in bed, he'd be as happy as a boy in love for the first time to watch Emanuela slowly putting on the inner finery that only a lover would ever see, then sitting before her dressing-table mirror to perform complicated and gradually triumphant operations with comb and make-up. He'd pour two glasses of champagne and lounge cheerfully about. Then she'd put on the outer finery that was for all the world, and she'd position the Tiepolo clusters in her hair and at her throat.

On bad days, although while she dressed Hugh would loll on her window-seat apparently with the same worldly equanimity as ever, he'd brood nervously that it was only his intoxication with her body that made him think she had uncommon talent as a singer, made him believe she might conceivably achieve her dream of singing great parts on famous stages. Then he'd follow this up by deciding that she probably knew perfectly well that she was never going to emerge from her provincial mediocrity at La Fenice, which was why she was sensibly on the look-out for an amiable, rich husband, or someone who would be, practically speaking, a husband. He'd haul up the bedroom awning and let in the brilliance, in order to distract himself from knowing that, in this Bohemian world where Emanuela and he were adrift, he was nothing but a successful man, she was nothing but a young beauty, they were condemned to delude and betray one another. He'd call down to their gondolier, who'd be drowsing in his black hull with his straw hat shadowing his voluminous moustache, to distract himself from longing to be able to rejoice in her with the old, sane, honourable combination of hot-blooded desire and cool-spirited detachment, or for that matter with the good sense and good taste she had every right to expect in him.

Each time they saw one another, there was more of Hugh's awareness that he was compelled to conceal from Emanuela, as he suspected that there was more of hers that she concealed from him. So deceit entered their relations from the outset, quite naturally.

What vicious circles these were! When for week after week his duties prevented him getting to Venice, Hugh's consciousness was poisoned with jealous imaginings. When he was back at Ca' Zante for a few days, and he was offering Emanuela his elbow so she could step into their gondola, with a cascade of misery debouching into his brain he'd remember how insistently while he'd been away he'd invented romantic stories of their future together in this city of hers, stories of preposterous innocence and hopefulness. By the time her foot was on the gunwale, his misery would have vanished. He'd have met her candid, lit-up eyes smiling at him. He'd have heard her giggle because a boat's wake was making her wobble. He'd have remembered how Philip when he'd met Violet had emerged into something new. It wasn't so damned miraculous as all that, it wasn't even all that rare, he'd remind himself stalwartly. For pity's sake, just because you'd been fraudulent in love long ago didn't mean you were condemned always to be fraudulent. But then as the gunwale went down an inch under Emanuela's weight, as she wavered and held his arm more firmly, fatally the undertow in Hugh's brain would drag him back into his past, into the wastes of his lost time, which were far more inexorable now than when those commonplace, disappointing minutes and years had been his present. All his experience with Elizabeth had taught him was that he had no knowledge of his heart whatsoever. Therefore any decision he took now was likely to be wrong, any love he felt was probably false.

Whenever Hugh despaired and was on the verge of chucking Emanuela, suddenly all his defeating thoughts would cease. His good spirits would return. His time passed with her would be sufficient to itself and be happy – except that soon afterward he'd be possessed by anxiety lest she should be about to chuck him.

When spring came, they discarded their boat's *felze*, that tiny black cabin for two which in winter protected from cold and rain, as well as making lovers admirably invisible, but in sunshiny weather would have been an intolerable encasement. On luminous evenings they'd tell their gondolier to take them slowly twisting and turning into the labyrinth of northern Venice, of Cannaregio, where Emanuela had been brought up only a few hundred yards from where she now lived. Emanuela would wear her strands of pearls high on her throat in the manner of Tiepolo's blondes. Along those sinuous backwaters from the Ghetto to the Miracoli, they were always happening on a quay that reminded her of a battle fought between the children of hostile alleys, so she'd smile with memory and tell her lover about that, and he'd half listen, utterly at peace, glancing at a vine reefed along a garden wall, at a niche from which the saint had long since been stolen and sold. Then an archway to a house would remind Emanuela of an old music teacher she'd liked who now was dead, or they'd glide below a window from which at dead of night a rope-ladder had been let down so a girl-friend of hers could escape to a skiff waiting below. Often the lovers dined at a restaurant. Afterward they were still out on the canals long after darkness had fallen and bats were flitting.

If they went back to Ca' Zante, they'd arrive at the water-steps where the lantern's yellowish light glistened on the black tideway slopping at the palace's jetty, on a strand of weed, on a rusty mooring chain. Hugh would step back a pace, still out of doors in the mild Grand Canal night, to watch Emanuela as she gave him a quick smile and entered the soundless, glimmering hall, its air just as brackish as the air outside but always cool.

If they had themselves rowed back to the flat at the Madonna dell'Orto, a night walker's tread might sound along the quay as they approached. Here and there Emanuela's neighbours would have brought oil lamps and kitchen chairs out beside the water. There'd be low, local voices. Vessels would nudge against mooring posts. Someone would toss a cigarette into the water. Someone else might call softly, 'Good night!' and Emanuela would answer, 'Good night!'

VII

During his years at Eton, Robert Mancroft had learned dislike of institutions and of the men and boys who flourished in them. He lay awake at night imagining the furze heath at Brack with its warrens where the gamekeeper took him ferreting, imagining the woods of oak and alder where on Christmas holiday afternoons his father took him to shoot pigeon, imagining the river in summer when a hatch of dragonflies would flit up over the thatched boathouse.

Then his father was killed, and at first the boy's grief was so simple and so utter that it felt like a cruel stupidity he'd got trapped in. He wanted to be riding his half-Arab pony beside his father over the Brack meadows, or rowing with him on the river, because only those canters and that clinker-built dinghy and those moments were happiness, and he knew that they were for ever impossible, so happiness was never going to come back, and the hated tears kept choking his throat and his brain, kept humiliating him. It was later, as month after month went by and no clemency evinced itself in the workings of the world, that he tormented himself by longing never to be conscious of his old home again. He even longed to be able to forget his father for a while, to have a rest from his misery, not always to be conscious of that one thing, and then for days he'd be red-eyed with self-loathing and with remembering.

In superficial fact Robert had not lost Brack as irrevocably as all that, because his elder half-brother and half-sister kept insisting that he must always spend as much time there with them as he wished. But in the course of one autumn he had entered that death-imbued state in which the soul haunts a lost place and time and happy love (his young mind grasped instinctively that these three were never to be disentangled). Brack and its woods and waterways had become a domain he would never possess again or cease to be possessed by. The sense of a lost rightness in the world, of its lost truth to himself, took up dominion over him, before he could resist it or yet be conscious of the slow, expanding, deleterious effects it would have on him.

By the time the Mancrofts' train was rushing and clanking east toward Verona through squalls of rain, Robert's relationship with his father had become a compulsive listening with his inner ear, so that he always seemed to know what the dead man would say to this or how he'd react to that. He was solitary, and forced to grow up too quickly, and this complicated his other primal, inescapable love, which was for his mother. He was responsible to his dead parent for his living one.

He never told his mother about the enshrined injustices at

Eton that he rebelled against, about the bullying and the flogging, about the traditions he found phoney and the *esprit de
corps* he found embarrassing, though he knew she knew he
didn't like the place. With the same desire not to hurt her,
he worried in silence about how she was no better than he
was, she too for days and nights was most alive in her lost
time with his father. Somehow to be able to be true to the
past while living with at least a nearly whole heart in the
present . . . He knew that his mother and he each felt this to
be impossible for themselves but longed for it for the other.
But how could it be arrived at?

Robert at his train window was wondering what sort of
family their hosts for this Easter holiday would prove to be
(he had not been in Venice since he was four, and had only
a couple of times met his Venetian godfather in England),
and wondering whether his English godfather, whom he often
saw, would be the same in Italy or different, when at a curve
of the line he caught a glimpse of storm-blurred bell-towers
far ahead, and at that moment the icy welter turned to the
last snow blizzard of the spring. Nearer than the black smoke
gouting up from the engine and being whipped tattering
away, gusts of glistening rain and gusts of white flakes pelted
in his sight, inextricable, seething across the remains of the
blossom in the orchards, across the maples and cedars in a
villa garden.

The boy's jutty-jawed, jutty-nosed face, with its freckles
and its sprouting brown hair, suddenly came to life, his greeny-
grey eyes shone. The sleet was already faltering. The sun
came out through rainy snow or snowy rain flying every

second more weakly, more sparsely, and in the sky beyond, panels of silvery grey and dark blue light appeared, with the last spangles of the deluge falling across them. His lips smiling and his eyes entranced, he looked at his mother sitting opposite him, but she was still reading her book.

Robert went back to wondering about Venice. Would it be like London had been as soon as his mother had stopped wearing black, where in restaurants with pillars and chandeliers a gentleman at another table might keep letting his glance flick in her direction, and then would murmur something to the friend he was lunching with? A brick and marble city on the sea, made of hundreds of islands hitched together with humpy bridges, where you went about by boat. But were there going to be dinner parties where Mummy responded vivaciously to the men on her left and her right? (Robert's prickly awareness of his mother as an object of desire was made more painful by his own all-pervading fascination with teenage girls.) Were there going to be men they'd only just been introduced to who'd say the most idiotic things to her, which they'd think were brilliant and which she wouldn't object to anything like enough? Oh *yes*, darling, she'd drawl afterward – or at least she would if he'd made her meet his look. I *did* notice, Robbie. *Aren't* people ridiculous?

'You've been to Verona before, but you were so little you've forgotten,' his mother was saying to him gaily, closing her novel and dropping it into her travelling bag. 'I remember how we tucked you up in the hotel with Nanny, and then Daddy and I went to the Roman amphitheatre to hear *Aida*.

A marvellous setting for it, of course, on a summer evening, and they'd got palm trees, and a sphinx, and camels . . . No, surely they *can't* have had camels, I must have invented that. That's what we'll do, we'll find out what music is being performed hereabouts. We'll go to the Fenice and look at the singers through those tiny opera glasses they give you. What fun!' she exclaimed, though a frown that he didn't understand had suddenly crinkled her forehead. 'Still, we'd better not gaze at them too closely, because the acting is usually embarrassing, the thing is to listen. What else? We'll go to St Mark's and hear the Gregorian chants. What do you say to that?'

And she gave him the bright, valiant smile that for several heartbeats he'd been waiting for, the smile that being enthusiastic about things that she'd done with his father always brought to her lips sooner or later, and that always afflicted him with oppression even before it came.

VIII

They had reached Verona. Happy to be distracted, Robert let his eyes swing across the edge of his mother's dark emerald dress on the worn maroon plush of the seat opposite him, past the brass fittings on the glass door of their compartment and a man in a bowler hat walking along the corridor, out to the station yard where in blustery sunshine a porter with a besom was sweeping shining water toward the runnels of a drain that appeared to be blocked. Passengers who had got off the train clambered into cabs and were driven away at a trot, the horses' wet hindquarters glistening below pollarded lime trees, their April pale green being belaboured by gusts. The driver of a motor cab held his crank up before his eyes a moment, as if to say, 'This excellent device will do the trick.' He strode around to the front of his machine's bonnet, bent over importantly, and prodded the crank into its socket. A boy drove up in a trap with a grey cob between the shafts, jumped down, unhooked a nose-bag from the tail-board and peered into it. When the train jolted forward and

Robert lost sight of him, he was patting his horse's neck with one hand, while with the other he reached up and pushed the leather strap of the nose-bag over its head.

When his mother had picked up her novel again, Robert looked at her – though for several seconds, with a multiplicity his imagination had always had and which therefore didn't surprise him, he was also still watching a rain-sleeked cob between varnished shafts that lowered its dappled head and snuffled the oats in its nose-bag. At the same time as he brooded about his mother (anxiety for her had become so recurrent that it was a fundamental condition of his life), he was murkily aware too that his imagination, with still more of the multiplicity that seemed to be natural to it, was getting ready for its next – what? – he didn't know, yet – but the new wondering would come – it was half alive already.

When people looked at Violet Mancroft these days, usually their eyes concluded that she was still nearly as beautiful as ever, or they noticed that, since her husband had been killed, traces of tense misery had begun to engrave themselves beside her mouth and her eyes.

What her son saw when he contemplated her was different, and strictly speaking had nothing to do with her appearance, which was so familiar and so loved by him as scarcely to be visible to his eyes.

From the slant of her neat hat, from her absorbed eyes as she read, from the curve of her chin, from the pair of mother-of-pearl earrings she was wearing, from a tiny motion of her lips as she finished a chapter and at once started the next ... From all these, which on another occasion might have been almost exactly the same and yet have yielded Robert quite different information, this afternoon he unerringly deduced that while they were in Venice she'd be reminded at every turn of being there with his father, but that this might be counterbalanced by her pleasure in introducing he himself to the place, so he must try hard to make this a success. He was reminded that his mother was, he had thought, uneasy about his godfather Hugh for some reason, or she was uneasy about seeing him this particular time – so he wanted to get to the bottom of this unsatisfactory state of affairs. He was reminded that his mother entertained hopes, so tenuous that she'd scarcely started to mention them to him, that Venice just possibly might be a more bearable city for her to go to earth in than London.

Robert was about to wonder about Venice as a place where you might bivouac for long enough for it to become a kind of surrogate home, when his attention was caught by a farmstead with high barns – they must have been hay barns – and a church that their train was hurtling past. The sky was serene now and, to judge by the trees, the wind was dying momently. An old woman was riding a donkey along a track, whacking its rump with her umbrella with a regular up and down of her arm.

Distracted, with a complete transfiguration of his thinking, Robert's restive mind sheered off, though not in the direction of the hay barns and the donkey. He began not simply to remember his father but, for the first time in his life, to ask himself about memory. *Why* did he go back to the lost? For what? When he went back to sailing *Calypso* down the coast with Daddy, or to wildfowling with him on winter dusks, what was the mysterious something that the past half rendered up to him and half did not? He wondered with seventeen-year-old precocity, passionately logical and at the same time tossed hither and thither by his passions and his dreams.

Sometimes he'd find that he'd vanished away to the past before he'd realised he was no longer in the present. Right, that was straightforward enough, he thought. But at other times the temptation would be too great, he'd be unable not to *choose* to let himself go haunting back, though he knew it was cruel and delusory, he knew that afterward he'd wake up dead-alive in the here and now. Well, perhaps Venice would be different, possibly Venice would change everything. In London a few days before, Mummy and he had prepared themselves for this journey by going to look at paintings by Canaletto. Perhaps in Venice waking up here and now would not always be a disappointment. There'd be palaces, and a girl who waved from a window as your boat drew near . . .

His chin on his fist by the train window, suddenly Robert let himself imagine the Brack woods encumbered with early summer leaf, low branches such impenetrable barricades and high branches such dense canopies above canopies that you were hemmed around by sun-dappled greens and shady greens. He imagined invisible wood-pigeons that cooed high up in the bowery stillness, the brilliant blue flash of a king-fisher as it darted along a stream.

His father and he had often gone in summer to check that the young trees they'd planted the previous winter and the winter before that were all right, and now they'd come back together ghostlily . . . Because that had been one of the rituals they'd shared. Was that why? And because this coming back might be horribly painful, but it was a misery that held all the richness of the world, or held its only paltry significance, or . . . Well, he decided, he'd keep faith, even if he didn't understand anything about it.

His father and he were wading slowly through the nettle-beds. They were using sticks to knock their way through bramble patches, through festoons of wild hops and bind-weed. High up, the pigeons' melody was continuous, and all around the warm air was a dance of motes of shadow and motes of light. They scrambled over a fallen alder, its trunk wrapped inches deep in ivy. A spider's web clung to his eyes and mouth, catkins got in his hair.

Other people thought his inability to shake himself free of his father's death was a weakness, he knew they did and he despised them for it. People thought too that endlessly haunting back was unhealthy or unmanly. Well, they could call it what they liked.

Burrs stuck to his clothes, he had a pale blob of cuckoo-spit on one shoe. Sweat wetting his shirt, he clambered through a thicket of elder, the last of its sprays of white flowers smelling sickly sweet, its clusters of berries still tight and green, not yet soft and moist and blackish red. 'About here, if I remember rightly,' his father said, puffing as he struggled through the elder beside him. 'Where that big chestnut came down, remember? We planted two or three young ones to fill the gap.'

They stood in the clearing that had been made by the fall

of a mighty horse-chestnut tree the previous year. The quiet was murmurous with insects, and through the opening in the tree-tops shimmery shafts of sunlight slanted down. The gale-wrecked chestnut had become a thicket of nettles which butterflies were flitting over, and was laced every-which-way by tough pinkish-green arms of over-arching brambles – but here was one of the little replacements they'd planted.

'Found one of them!' he exclaimed happily, and set to work with his stick bashing the greenery away from the short, thin sapling which otherwise the summer's undergrowth would smother. 'It's been a bit hampered by all this goose-grass, but it'll be all right.' He reached out his grubby, scratched fingers to touch the little chestnut's sticky tip.

'Oh Robbie, my poor darling,' his mother said, leaning toward him in the carriage and putting her hand on his knee. 'Here, borrow my handkerchief. Heavens, we're as bad as each other, you and I.'

Robert arrived in Venice upset and distracted, having utterly lost his hopes of what the place might be and might offer.

IX

The day before the Mancrofts' arrival, Hugh Thurne had just got back to Ca' Zante from Paris, where since early in the year he'd been one of the delegates at the Peace Conference. He was waiting for Emanuela Zuccarelli, who had promised him that she would come this evening. He was also trying, as he phrased it, to knock some sense into his own head. This whole business of attempting to put his life in order, or rather to order his thoughts so that this might in due course have the desired effect upon his life, had been given urgency by his wish to devote himself with a peaceful mind to Violet and her son for these few days over Easter, but it was not going well.

He was in the walled garden, which from one minute to the next had convinced him as a place where his wits might have a chance of winning at least a few of their tussles with their own obduracy — or if not, well, anyhow, at least this gravel path was a pleasant place to fret to and fro, what with the medlar tree, and the persimmon tree, and the roses on trellises. The trouble was that, instead of reasoning his way steadily forward, resolving his perplexities one after another and arriving at sensible conclusions, he kept pulling his watch out of his fob pocket. He was continually being distracted by how irresistible the sight of Emanuela would be if by some miracle she was early and suddenly was there before his eyes under the arbour, and then being distracted far worse by sensual imaginings of the night to come, all of which made him feel absurdly cheerful and not logical at all.

Emanuela's sister Tiziana, before she'd married that fat count of hers in the armaments racket, had worked her way through a fair number of superficial liaisons with well-off men. Hugh knew this because he'd been one of them. Part of the disgraceful charm of his first seduction of Emanuela a year later had been that of having the younger sister too.

This wretched inconvenient fact, which since his feelings for Emanuela had become so tender had bothered him dreadfully (though luckily she had never seemed the slightest bit concerned about it), had yet again obtruded itself into his musing. Flopping down on the garden bench but then at once standing up again to resume his slow, long-legged, meditative stalking along the gravel, with a prodigious mental effort Hugh resolved that his having passed a few afternoons in bed with Tiziana might be horribly regrettable but it was also irrelevant to the decision he had very nearly come to. And this decision was going to be that . . . Yes, but why, each time that he tried to put Emanuela together in his head, did she fall to pieces? There was Emanuela the Lido good-time girl. There was Emanuela the admirably modern, independent young woman for whom 'good-time girl' would be an insult. There was Emanuela whose passion was opera, which unfortunately was the one art form he'd never been very good at taking seriously, but never mind. On and on it went, the rigmarole; on and on it went, his thinking and thinking until he knew he didn't understand anything. He'd fallen in love with her, not in his heart which was far too worldly and knowing, but in his imagination – yes, that was it! Like the commonplace middle-aged susceptible idiot that he was, he'd dreamed up his image of a Tiepolo girl, and there she'd been, perfect, incomparable. Well, maybe now he was going to be saved, because since she'd bobbed her hair she'd been looking a lot less Tiepolo than before.

Swinging around because he'd reached the persimmon tree again, Hugh clenched his mind onto the necessity of coming to a clear, irrevocable decision. Then he halted. He gazed toward the gate where his imagination had brought Emanuela into being as if she'd just that minute arrived, wavering for a couple of heartbeats in the dapple beneath the wisteria till her eyes found him and she quickened her step.

Smiling ruefully, Hugh started back down the path, swinging his malacca stick. No, she couldn't possibly be here for another hour. In the meanwhile, even if Elizabeth and he ever agreed to go their separate ways . . . Even if Emanuela and he then went to the cumbersome lengths of getting married . . . That wouldn't mean that she was his, or mean that he would find a happiness he'd never found in the past. It would merely demonstrate, to any of their acquaintances who might be interested, quite how weak-willed and avid they both were. It'd show the lengths to which he'd go to fix himself up with a beguiling young – what? – concubine, that was probably the accurate word. It would show that what mattered to Emanuela rather more than Verdi and Wagner, and mattered rather more than true love, was a future of affluence, idleness, luxury, in which she would in time naturally hope for a family.

No, that was all rubbish! *Why* did he keep fooling himself? Elizabeth and he weren't going to get divorced. For good or ill, they weren't those sorts of people, it was out of the question. Now that they saw each other so infrequently, they'd been getting on more pleasantly, or less unpleasantly, than they had for years. And whatever else you might say about this bad joke of a marriage, it was the least atrocious option for their boys. So . . . So the honourable thing to do was to ditch Emanuela, to set her free. Then one fine day she could marry someone far more suitable.

At the medlar tree once more, he stood leaning on his stick, frowning wryly, glancing up at the April brilliance in the new leaves, listening to the creak of an oar as a boat passed along the subsidiary canal on the other side of the wall. Oh but to hell with it – he wasn't going to ditch Emanuela quite yet – he couldn't! – why should he? And for God's sake, she was old enough to stand on her own two feet. Just look at this fantastic light! How could you give anything up that was living, that was here, that was now? And when the time came to say goodbye, which it fatally would before all that long, he'd wish her well with the same ironic heart with which she'd wish him well, and with the

same hardly diminished liking, and with the same amusement scarcely tinged with regret.

It was the housekeeper, not Emanuela Zuccarelli, who was
approaching him from the *pietra d'Istria* arch into the house,
carrying his letters on a salver. Recognising an old London
friend's handwriting on one of the envelopes, he opened it
first.

*My dear Hugh, I'm sure you won't take it amiss if I
... Several of us have been thinking that at least you
should be alerted – and that heron's head of yours is
always stuck so high up in the clouds that even those
of us who've known you for years haven't a clue what
you've noticed and what you haven't ... Rather more
serious than possibly you're aware ... Before the year
is out, I'm afraid you could easily find yourself being
asked if you object to your gloriously unconjugal behaviour being used by her lawyers to set her free ... Sorry
if I'm telling you something you already know. One
final thing. Not sure whether I ought to mention this,
but I'll risk it. I'm not the only one of Elizabeth's and
your friends who can't help being rather pleased for
her. Of course she's being very level-headed. But her
eyes have a shine they haven't had for a long time.*

Standing under the arbour, the letter still in his hand,
Hugh Thurne flung his head up in delight at the liberty he
might be about to receive, and also in laughter at himself
because his mind was already tumbling with all manner of

possibilities that he'd repeatedly tried not to be enchanted by.

The birdsong all around him made it perfectly plain how straightforward and how good it was going to be to shrug off all that had gone before. (And whatever straits Emanuela had been reduced to during the war, when the theatres were closed, she'd be hard put to it to have a past as disreputable as his to consign to oblivion, that was for sure.) The chirruping and the fluting sang to him of how she and he would linger here arm in arm, April after April (well, why not?), their spirits freed from old oppression, contented to do unimportant, vital things such as take pleasure in the finches busybodying in the ivy on the canal wall where they had a nest. The blue flowers on the dark green rosemary were an evident proof of how often and how merrily his sons and his godson would come to this house for their holidays. Above him, it was manifest from the greyish blue sun-shot air that Emanuela, almost without doubt, entertained the same dreams as he did.

Hugh took a few impulsive strides and perched himself on the stone rim of the small, dribbly fountain (the pump needed to be repaired) with its smell of damp ferns, swinging one leg gaily and stuffing the abruptly folded letter into the breast pocket of his suit.

The nitty-gritty of diplomatic toil – so exclusively grounded in national interests, so eloquent of human chicanery, truly just year after year of the astute wording of ambiguous pronouncements, year after year of coming away from every conversation having taken more than you'd given . . . Oh, of course he didn't mind confessing that he'd been disgustingly ambitious in his day, but latterly it had been wearying him. Honestly it would be rather a relief to step aside from the obsession with career that was a perfectly acceptable occupation for second-rate minds. He'd found himself being tempted by these new possibilities and new freedoms again only quite recently. Naturally a man in Philip Mancroft's inherited position in society, and for that matter a man of Philip's cheerfully implacable self-confidence, had been able to chuckle contemptuously at those who'd presumed to find his conduct or his divorce unbecoming. But he himself – well, his Foreign Office career would be scuppered by a scandal such as this would be, and no mistake. Oh, what the hell! How sensible to ask them: please, would they pension him off? What, like an old steeplechaser put out to grass? Yes – exactly like that. That would do splendidly. His interests in history and world affairs would become at once more abstract, more profound, and (this was obvious now that he'd thought of it for the first time in his life) a source, very simply, of intellectual delight. Emanuela and he would travel a lot. Whole days would pass when he'd do nothing but read and muse.

So Emanuela's and his attractiveness to one another was deplorably superficial, was that the problem? (Dizzied by his gaiety, he ran one hand over the moist moss on the carved stonework beside him.) So it was just erotic pleasure dolled up with romanticism and made tawdry by a few of the common sorts of self-interest, it was the oldest story in the world, did shrewd people reckon? Well, of course it was! –

but men and women were what they were, you had to work with the materials that came to hand. As to whether for the rest of his days he was going to have to pretend that opera could be spoken of in nearly the same breath as the higher arts . . . Well, so be it – and for pity's sake, there were always prices to pay, the thing was to find it amusing.

Now, the absolute priority was that Emanuela and he should stop pretending that this was just another amorous adventure or amusing interlude or what-have-you. They must stop playing by rules that didn't apply. For a start, it was high time he asked about her parents (they were still alive in her old home in Ruga Do Pozzi, but that was all he knew about them), and high time he introduced her to – well, to the Veniers, for example.

Swinging himself off the fountain, Hugh lit a cheroot.

He knew that any moment now he'd be mortified that he could even contemplate turning his sons' lives topsy-turvy just because their mother had taken a fancy to some brigadier or other, or because he himself couldn't be at peace unless he got his hands onto Emanuela at nice regular intervals – he knew all that . . . But just for a minute it was terrific to feel younger and more vigorous and more fired up by possibility than he had for years, and these new Dutch cheroots he'd recently been buying really were an excellent smoke, especially when for a whole bunch of deplorable reasons you were smiling more impetuously than you had since you could remember. Young! That was a joke. He'd be fifty in a couple of years.

Hugh propped his shoulder luxuriously against one of the uprights of the arbour.

Above all, even if it took some time for a divorce to be achieved, or even if that mere legal detail were never achieved, Emanuela and he must begin to be more open and more loving with one another. Oh Lord, why had he left this until now, when for a few days he really would have no option but to devote himself to Violet and her son? And immediately after that he had to leave for London. Well, never mind! The essence of it was that Emanuela must soon, she must tonight, she must again tomorrow morning, be aware of greater candour, greater confidence, greater possibility.

Oh yes – and another thing. This was a lot more vital than whether they spent years and years together or they didn't, or whether he ever became ambassador in Rome.

X

The following morning Emanuela had a rehearsal at the Fenice, to which Hugh had offered to accompany her, before in the afternoon he went to meet the Venier family and the new arrivals from England.

The lovers were both in the softened mood that always followed their nights together. Fusillades of rain had drubbed against the windows while they were getting dressed and drinking their coffee. Then the sky had cleared. Over the marshes in the lagoon, the larks had winged up into the bright, towering air. In the island villages and in the city, men crouched in their barges and their skiffs had started to bail, their tin scoops knocking against the bilges, then the scoops and the flung rainwater glittering. Coming out at the water-gate at Ca' Zante, Emanuela raised one hand to shade her eyes, because the sunlight along the Grand Canal was a cobwebby dazzle of wetness and brilliance, and because as usual during her nights at Ca' Zante she'd drunk more wine than she was accustomed to and hadn't slept quite enough.

Hugh had been delayed for a minute, by the housekeeper. Holding onto the rail so she didn't slip on the soaked planks, and still feeling drowsy, Emanuela stepped onto the jetty, where their gondolier was waiting for them, a new man whom she already didn't like on account of his appraising, amused eyes every time he saw her.

'Good morning!' she said in her most forthright voice, and at once thought: Dear God, surely the brute could do more than grunt, couldn't he? And it *is* offensive, the way he looks at me – it's horrible!

Emanuela self-consciously buttoned up her navy blue mackintosh, looking down her front and making a method-ical job of it. She buckled its belt around her waist with a slight jerk. For some reason the gulls' cries sounded un-naturally loud in her ears, and below her feet the blinding ripples made her eyes flinch and her brain waver. She glanced resolutely across the tideway to the rinsed facades and the shining window-panes opposite, and she was about to go back into the house to fetch Hugh when he appeared, hurriedly pulling on his coat at the same time as he clapped his trilby onto his head.

'Sorry about that! Not only do we have a drain that at some unidentified spot in the innards of this house has got blocked, we've also got rain in the attic. You know, where they hang up the laundry to dry. Right, let's go. Lord, it's bright out here!'

'It makes my head feel dizzy!' exclaimed Emanuela happily, the sight of Hugh and the sound of his voice at once making her limbs feel deliciously languorous again (which the insolent gondolier had only put them off feeling for a minute), and making her mind go back to being the most languorous bit of her of all. 'This jetty is on its last legs, I've been telling you for months. Hang onto me, I'm about to fall in, and if I have to go upstairs again to change then I'll really be late. All this wine we always end up drinking! Not to mention the other dreadful things we stay awake to do.'

'Oh, I think mussels and bream that good call for something decent to wash them down. What happens if people are late for these rehearsals of yours?'

She giggled. 'The punishments – I can't tell you, they're so wonderful! That's why some of us are always drifting in long after we were meant to.'

Snuggling into her seat in the gondola, Emanuela for a moment remembered the ill-mannered oarsman standing high behind her, but only in order to decide that she'd simply tell Hugh to get rid of him. Then she forgot the lout completely. Her tired, sensual, contented mind picked on an image here and a notion there, with an inconsequentiality that was its own inconsequentiality and therefore felt comfortable. This love affair that went on and on – the famous conductor Della Rovere who was about to begin a season here – how these days, thank the Lord, she never had to worry about money – her new shantung silk dress, with its sash slung low around her hips – the Hotel Excelsior and the Hotel des Bains, which before long would open for the summer . . . All these lulled her. What was more, it was a great improvement to be winding through the crooked canals toward the theatre, rather than slogging there on foot all the way from Cannaregio as she'd generally used to. Hugh truly was a sweetheart – she'd have found out long ago if underneath he was different from how he appeared. Now, what was it that she was going to have to wake up sufficiently to sing today? And just think if . . . No, he was married, poor darling – married to some English frump who was ghastly to him. Well, you didn't have to be married. And Papa and Mamma would finally have to agree that . . . Oh look, Giovanna and Tonino must have been evicted at last – that was their house, with handcarts outside piled up with kit. What bastards landlords were!

None of Hugh Thurne's perplexities had been resolved, but he was in such idle, magnanimous spirits this morning and his thoughts were so agreeably disconnected, like his lover's, that nothing seemed to matter very much. So Elizabeth, who was one of the most hidebound women he'd ever met, was so enamoured that she was prepared to contemplate the scandal of a divorce – heavens, fancy that! (He glanced sideways at Emanuela's profile as she was borne past a dilapidated palace wall, at her cloche hat, at the velvet choker high on her throat.) And all their friends in England were already assuming that, seeing as how for years and years he'd been as neglectful and as unfaithful as it was possible for a husband to be, of course now he'd have to do the decent thing and raise no objections. So whether the scandal broke or it didn't, and therefore whether his diplomatic career was consigned to the dustbin or it wasn't, were already out of his control! The whole damned shooting match depended on whether Elizabeth lost her nerve at the last minute, or whether Bill Knox ever noticed that her conversation was one banality after another . . . though come to think of it, maybe it was her fortune he was after – and she'd be a fair bit richer again when her father died. Really, you had to see the funny side of it all.

When they reached the Fenice, at the water entrance the tall doors had been opened, a barge had been tied up, and workmen were unloading painted screens. At some water-steps beneath a colonnade, Hugh stood up in the gondola to help Emanuela ashore. But then he lingered, steadying himself with one hand on a marble bollard, still holding her with his eyes, because she was so glorious hesitating there above him before she turned away, and he'd remembered his resolutions of the previous evening. On an impulse, he jumped up onto the quay and took a few paces beside her so they were out of earshot of their gondolier.

'Emanuela, don't vanish into thin air just because my English friends are going to be in town! Honestly, the way you and I tiptoe discreetly around each other's independence is almost too much of a good thing. Couldn't we . . . ? Oh, I don't know, but . . . Listen, I've been wanting you to meet Giacomo and Valentina Venier for ages. If I invite the Mancrofts and them for lunch tomorrow or the next day, will you come?'

'Oh, I can't speak English, I mean not really, and . . .' Her hands shoved down into the pockets of her mackintosh, she cocked her head a little to one side as she smiled at him, her eyes kindled, amused, wondering. 'You'll have news you want to catch up with. You'll have a far merrier time if you don't have to bother about bringing me into the conversation.

Goodbye! Tell me when you're next free. Oh, and . . . Last night was wonderful.'

Not in the least dismayed by Emanuela's refusal (he was sure from her eyes that she would accept this sort of suggestion before long, and that the deepening and widening of their tenderness would be possible), Hugh sat beside her empty seat as he was rowed home. It was one of those merciful days when the past ceased to be an oppression, the future couldn't conceivably be worth upsetting yourself about, and all that he didn't know about Emanuela was more amusing than it was anything else. Whether during the war her sister and she had made much of a habit of passing their men to each other; what she got up to when he was the other side of town, let alone the other side of Europe; whether the rumour was true that some of them at the Fenice were quite cheerful about taking their pleasure for half an hour in the dressing-rooms with any of their fellow performers they'd taken a shine to or with a newcomer they liked the look of . . . This morning all these questions made Hugh smile to himself and cross one ankle over the other knee as he was rowed back to the Grand Canal, and made him muse that even after years, you'd be pretty hazy about much of a lover's thinking and doing and feeling, and a good job too. He screwed up his eyes against the radiance of the morning, so he could focus on the porphyry roundels on the facade of his house as he drew near. Emanuela the Bohemian girl accountable to no one; Emanuela probably the good Catholic daughter too . . . If the truth were known, the high point of each week for her was probably when she trotted home to her parents, and stirred the polenta for the family's Sunday lunch. Hang on – what was this damned oarsman muttering about?

'Excellency, seeing that you like blondes, I could easily supply you with a few others.'

Fury jolted through Hugh's brain. Above him and behind him, the voice resumed: 'Beautiful, young girls.'

The maddening thing about needing to snarl at a gondolier was that you had to wrench around in your seat by a hundred and eighty degrees and then gaze up at him where, high above you, he swayed elegantly at his oar. Or possibly this was the saving thing, because although Hugh's neck throbbed, his face was discoloured, and his eyes (alas, he was sure of this) showed his hurt for Emanuela, in a matter of instants his self-possession and his sense of humour returned to him. Without snarling anything, he flopped back in his seat facing forward again, aware of the man looking down at the top of his hat and no doubt smiling, but no longer in danger of reacting to this. 'You're fired,' he said languidly.

Back on the Ca' Zante jetty, Hugh paid the gondolier what he owed him. Doubling it by way of a final tip, and making himself look the man civilly in the eyes, he said cheerfully: 'I'm sorry, but I don't believe that Signorina Zuccarelli and I will need you any longer.' Then he strode blithely indoors to tell them that he'd require a new boat that afternoon.

One of the upshots of Hugh Thurne's life having been a combination of relentless sociability and equally durable solitude was that he rather enjoyed lunching or dining alone, so long as he never had to do this too regularly. Chuckling at what a fool he'd been to be outraged even for a moment when a poor devil of a gondolier (half of them were pimps – for pity's sake, everybody knew that!) had made an assumption that the apparent facts most amply justified, he went to the kitchen in excellent spirits to enquire if it would be possible, at one o'clock, to have a couple of artichokes, please, or something like that, and an omelette, and that was all. Then he went upstairs to the library to write letters, suddenly pleased that for a few hours he had his house and his consciousness to himself, after the departure of his lover and before he got involved with his impending friends. He answered all his recent correspondents, briskly and adequately, except for the one writer who called for a thought-out response – but how could you reply even to the nicest fellow in all London if you hadn't yet got the foggiest notion what to say to him? – and went down to the dining-room with a good appetite.

The artichokes, the eggs and even the bread tasted first-rate, and so did his glass of Pinot Grigio.

The dining-room was on the first floor, with windows over the garden and over the side canal – windows that today let in so much sunlight that no lamps had been lit. Hugh sat at the head of the polished table, enjoying the shimmer in the long room, enjoying the quietness of the house all around him, and remembering that, with Giacomo so unwell these days that his professional life must be just about over, the Venier family's finances were going to be more precarious than ever. A year or two ago, Valentina appeared to have put her insomnia behind her, but now quite likely she'd have gone back to lying awake at night. Francesco was still only in his first year at the university, and hadn't so far shown much dedication to anything except boats by day and parties at night, which of course was as it should be. Even so, it wasn't too soon to introduce the lad to a few people who might, when the time came, put him on useful paths – and in Rome too, not only in Venice, in Rome where the clout and the money were going to be. This was the sort of thing he *could* do for his old friends and their son. And in London, in due course, if he could give Philip's boy a helping hand he'd do that too.

1797 . . . They'd ended up talking about 1797 when he'd dined with the Veniers a couple of months ago, and quite likely they would again tonight. Hugh smiled, making a vague bet with himself as to the odds of the fall of Venice cropping up. Valentina wasn't so bad. But Giacomo was one of the educated men of this defunct city state who still hadn't got over the senescence of their empire, who couldn't stop fretting over the political and military feebleness of those last unforgivable years. He talked well about it all, too. About the armed forces and the fighting spirit that, from the earliest interweavings of mankind's stories to the latest, all peoples had needed if they were to defend themselves, if they were to keep their freedom. About the whole troublous business of how high civilisations only seemed to grow when you had political independence, and if you lost that, or you got into the habit of compromising it, decline would follow, sure as fate. Giacomo had a whole parade of decaying imperial powers and decaying civilisations, from glory days and twilights in Greece and Persia and Arabia onward, that he liked to cheer himself up by ruminating over.

Deciding abruptly that Giacomo Venier would be precisely the right person to coax into coming with them on some of the historical and art-historical excursions he was planning for Robbie Mancroft (for instance in the northern lagoon, where they'd put on boots and plod around in the Torcello quagmires), Hugh finished his omelette, broke off a final piece of bread and refilled his glass.

Of course, since Violet had been widowed he'd neglected her and her son shamefully, what with work, and his love affair, and one thing and another. But now he was going to put that to rights.

'Your new flame' – that was how Violet would refer to Emanuela. Oh, she knew something was up – of course she did!

Discovering that he had shoved back his chair, crossed his legs, frowned, and taken a quite unnecessarily hearty swig of his wine, without having consciously intended to do a single one of these things, Hugh set his glass firmly back on the table, annoyed with himself for having felt a moment's uneasiness. Well, conceivably it wasn't such a bad thing that Emanuela had declined to come to lunch. All things in their good time. And right now, over Easter, he was going to concentrate on his godson. Heavens, poor old Philip . . . These days he practically never thought of him.

XI

Everybody in the Venier household was preparing to welcome Violet Mancroft and her son in their own fashion, some more practically than others.

Thanks to the war, and thanks to the country's and the family's economic difficulties, Elena was the only person who still worked for Giacomo and Valentina Venier, though when she had started ten years before there had been another maid as well as herself. There'd been a cook, there'd been a laundress. There'd been Sergio the gondolier who, when he wasn't rowing anybody anywhere, had cranked water up from the well, had carried firewood, had mended shutters and repainted them – he'd done all manner of odd jobs, before he got too old. In those days, no member of the family had ever put their hand to any housework at all. Elena had even heard tell of times when a far bigger establishment than that had been maintained, a hundred years ago maybe, she wasn't sure when. A valet and a seamstress, a tutor and a governess, footmen, half a dozen maids instead of only two ... A good place to work, in those days, it must have been.

Now in preparation for the visitors she had been sweeping and dusting rooms that customarily were never opened, and cleaning windows, and polishing furniture with beeswax. And she had been planning how most astutely to begin her manoeuvres, which would absolutely oblige the family to take on her cousin Donatella to help her with all the house-work. Donatella was still only twenty-five, but she had been afflicted by a succession of tragedies that, even by the stan-dards of those calamitous times, had caused her to be pitied in all the parishes round about, in the alleys behind San Marcuola where most of her relations lived, in the shops and boatyards along Santa Fosca. Both her little boys had died, the first a month after he was born, the other when he was three, of typhus. Then a few weeks after Caporetto her husband had died of his wounds. He'd died in a field hospital, they hadn't even been able to bring him home to the damp rooms along Rio San Felice where now Donatella couldn't pay the rent. Elena had no doubt that the Virgin Mary and the blessed saints would in time bestow holy balm upon Donatella's tortured heart, and it was equally plain to her that the Veniers must provide her with a job and a roof.

Valentina, helped in a distracted fashion by Gloria, had made the visitors' beds. She had set bunches of jonquils and crocuses (brought in from islands in the lagoon by ancient women and sold under neighbouring archways) on their dressing-tables. She had stuck handsome sprays of pear blossom into the Roman vase on the marquetry table in the *sala*.

This attempt to spruce up her damp, unhelpful palace, with its chipped paintwork and its faded furnishings, had produced its usual effect of making Valentina obscurely alarmed for her children's future. Given impulse by this, and once more dragooning Gloria into being her assistant, she had sallied forth yesterday to Rialto market, and this morning to the stalls along San Leonardo, so that at least the larder should be amply stocked with raw materials when great skills were expected of Elena at the kitchen range, and also so that her daughter should be in no doubt that even cloudy-headed girls were going to have to learn how much a veal cutlet or a bunch of asparagus cost, and learn to be responsible, and to have expectations that weren't too dreamy.

It was now half past four in the afternoon. Valentina felt exhausted already. She had a flustered idea that Francesco and Gloria, who were planning their own welcome for the guests from England, had already told her when the Mancrofts' train would arrive at the station, but she couldn't remember what they'd said, and right this minute she didn't particularly feel like being teased for having forgotten. Also, the labour in the dusty house and the fact that she hadn't seen Violet since before the war, when Philip had been as splendidly alive as a man could be, had combined to remind her of Donatella, and of Elena's plot, which was already dreadfully obvious, to have her enrolled here as a second woman-of-all-work.

Valentina was desperately sorry for Donatella – more sharply in anguish for her, perhaps, than her cousin was, on account of having more imagination and less confidence in the efficacy of the heavenly hosts in a case such as this. All the same, despite their attempts to be frugal, Giacomo had already been forced to sell a couple of paintings, as his father before him had sold statuary and furniture and silver, merely so that they could settle some rather pressing bills. So how could they possibly take on the responsibility of paying a second housekeeper's wages?

They could offer Donatella a bedroom, and they could feed her, of course they could – Valentina made herself remember that this was perfectly within their scope. But if she gradually began to be a help rather than a parasite, sooner or later she would have to be paid something, however beggarly. And once she came into the household, it was immensely unlikely that she would ever leave. Darling Francesco might have to support her all his life! Was it fair to saddle him with this?

The other thing was that although this house would be quite inconceivable without Elena's roundabout, blonde, hearty presence, and her sensible way of getting on with the jobs she had time for, and her even more commendable way of never making a silly fuss about all the things that didn't get done, Donatella's three mortal blows had left her like a woman whose soul had been taken from her. After suffering so much, and still suffering so much, she hardly reacted to anything. She didn't speak. Her eyes were dull, meaningless. Valentina knew it was a wrong thing to think, but even so, she couldn't help wondering whether she wanted this presence in her house for years and years, for ever probably.

The other day, Valentina had come into the kitchen to find

that Elena had brought Donatella without so much as a word
to anybody and had set her to work chopping up vegetables
– oh, the campaign had started all right, most definitely it
had started! Gloria had been there too, lending a hand. And
it had been more than Valentina could bear to think that
there might only be ten years between the girl and the young
woman, yet there was a chasm between what they had each
lived through. Standing shoulder to shoulder at the scrubbed
table, Gloria and Donatella had chopped more and more
slowly, both of them, quite oblivious that Elena and she herself had suddenly become unable to do anything except set
aside their own tasks and watch these two who had become
possessed – Valentina didn't have a clue by what – by something dreadful, something far too powerful to shake off. Then
any further hacking of carrots and courgettes, however clumsy
and slow, had clearly been out of the question. They'd laid
down their knives. Yes, her darling Gloria too! – Gloria who'd
never been anything other than irrepressible all her days until
that day. They'd stood with their hips against the table, gazing
into one another's faces, Donatella with her dead look, Gloria
with wide, wondering and then appalled eyes.

Valentina plumped down on a chair in the *sala*, to rest her
legs, and to try to forget about Donatella, and to wonder:
how would Violet be, after these terrible years, and after
Philip's death?

Giacomo might be alarmingly unwell but he hadn't been
killed, Valentina reminded herself sturdily. And luckily
Francesco's birthday fell at just the right time, and the war
had ended just in time, so it had been possible to pack him

off to the university rather than to a training camp. Honestly, what were her troubles, compared to Violet's? This house might be in a lamentable state of disrepair, so that for years it had been a family joke that the old place couldn't collapse to left or right on account of their neighbours' more robust masonry, which reduced the problem considerably, reduced it by precisely fifty per cent, because the house could only topple backward into the alley or forward into the Grand Canal. But at least she hadn't been turfed out of her home, unlike Violet. And if you went farther back . . . Gloria hadn't died when she was a baby, unlike Clementine, who would have been – what? – about thirteen, now, if she had lived.

Yes, but Violet herself . . . (Valentina raised her hands to rub her temples, trying to think effectively about her friend, and not have her tired head merely be awash with boring thoughts about the price of oysters, or about napery that in sunlight you could see perfectly well was stained.) Violet . . . Was she muffling her fatherless son with too many of the self-indulgent forms of love, so that she could feel more or less all right because she still adored, she could still be seen by others and by herself to adore and to devote herself self-lessly to, the person closest to her and most vulnerable to her? Was she letting herself be supported by Robert too much, and a good few years prematurely what was more, so that the poor lad was compelled to be nearly a man when perhaps it would have been more natural for him still to be a boy? Or was she getting some of these vilely difficult balances about right? And the inner woman herself: the whole, labyrinthine, lost woman . . . Philip's being killed would have

broken utterly vital things in her, Violet was far too loving
and far too true a person for that not to have occurred. But
in what ways, of all the possible sad ways? Had she got
wilder, or had she lost what had been that rather irresistible
vein of wildness? Would a second husband be acceptable one
day?

Francesco and Gloria had decided that the visitors from
England, as they were rowed from the railway station to the
house, should be met half-way not only by themselves in their
gondola but also by Hugh Thurne in his. (Francesco could
only recollect the Mancrofts vaguely, and Gloria had no
memory of them at all. The principal excitement, so far as
they were concerned, was that all this would entail seeing Sir
Hugh several times, who was a great favourite of theirs and
who didn't come to dinner anything like often enough.) For
this happy surprise in the middle of the Grand Canal to be
successfully stage-managed, it was necessary to calculate how
long the Mancrofts would take to get their luggage and themselves aboard a gondola and be rowed as far as the church
of San Geremia, or thereabouts, and it was also necessary to
know whether their train was running late, or even had been
cancelled as a lot of trains were these days, thanks to all the
political agitation on the mainland.

To discover this, Francesco had hurried off on foot to the
railway station, where the telegraphist had assured him that
the express had left Verona roughly on time and must now
be approaching Vicenza, and had let him use the telephone
to communicate this fact to Hugh Thurne's establishment.
(In Francesco's house, where water was still carried upstairs

89

in buckets, there was no telephone. But the owner of Ca'
Zante, as well as keeping the palace in good repair and keeping
it well staffed, had also thought to equip it with such modern
comforts as a marble bathroom with brass taps, and such
new-fangled gadgets as a telephone, in order to secure the
loyalty of well-heeled tenants like the present incumbent.)
Unfortunately on Francesco's way home again he had been
waylaid by a friend. Now he was in a café playing billiards,
continually glancing at the clock and announcing that he
must be on his way.

Just as Valentina Venier in the drawing-room on the first
storey dropped her fingers from her temples, stood up firmly,
and walked toward the kitchen with her alert step that never
varied even when she was tired, her husband arrived home
from his office. He was under the impression that he had
stumped along steadily and now was punctual for Violet and
her boy, but in fact he'd ambled wheezily as he always did,
stopping to admire a cornice that had given him pleasure all
his life, and stopping again at a bookshop. Then he'd stopped
a third time to talk to an old eel-man whom he could recall
coming to the house to sell to his mother's cook, and who
still trudged from quay to quay with a yoke across his shoulders and two pails of slowly writhing, slowly dying eels.

Giacomo let himself in through the massive street door
and stood still, beneath the dank, grimy beams and the unlit
chandelier, waiting for his fat chest to feel as if it had some
air and some strength in it, waiting till in the dimness his
eyes had focused on the Ionic columns, on the gate at the far
end where the rumpled Grand Canal gleamed. He took off

his overcoat. He took off his hat, and raised an automatic hand to smooth the white bristle on his big-boned head. But then for a minute he did nothing else.

Walking home, he'd been looking forward to seeing Violet, and he'd been recalling Philip, with whom he'd first become friends back in the eighties when they'd both been boys, and old Mr and Mrs Mancroft had spent three months at the Danieli Hotel. But now it came back to him yet again: Philip had fought for his country. He'd fought in the Near East, under General Allenby. He'd fought in the Middle East. When the call came, the man had answered; he'd offered his life and it had been taken.

Whereas he ... No army could conceivably have wanted him as an officer, or for that matter as a soldier either. God damn it, he wouldn't even have been up to digging latrines all day. The only question of any interest would have been whether, after say half an hour of that unexceptional duty, he made the other men laugh by fainting corpulently at their feet or released them from further encumbrance by having a heart-attack. Well, maybe he would just about have been up to being a quartermaster, making lists and ticking things off.

A fleshy lawyer, and not even a particularly successful one. A man who'd spent the war fretting about how neither of his children seemed to try very hard at school. A man who, when his country was invaded, had gone on shoving sheets of paper across a desk; who blinked at his clients through his spectacles, and thought carefully before he gave courteous, unimpeachable advice ...

No! The comparison was idiotic, it made no sense to make

it – how often had he told himself that? Philip had been a horseman and a yachtsman, he'd been as hard as nails – as well as being bloody rich from the minute he'd been born, and fortunate enough to be rich in a currency that when he'd been killed had still been worth something. Of course he'd been colonel of a yeomanry regiment – it was inconceivable that he shouldn't have been! – and of course he'd done it, you didn't have to say brilliantly, but beyond a shadow of doubt creditably. Like it or not, that was the sort of fellow he was.

Giving himself an irritable shake, and unbuttoning the jacket of his double-breasted suit, Giacomo remembered the dead man the last time he'd seen him, in London that Whitsun of '14, when they'd gone to lunch together at the Liberal Club. Oh, Philip Mancroft hadn't been any sort of a politician, thank God. But all the same, after he'd to all intents and purposes inherited that east-coast constituency, he'd always seemed to know what Asquith was going to say in the House the following day. He'd enjoyed being on the fringes of all that damned power that reached right around the globe and came back to the Greenwich meridian again. A fine time they'd had of it, the English of Philip Mancroft's stamp, until the war, when they'd become a bit more like everyone else.

Coughing, he walked upstairs.

XII

Gloria had explained meticulously to her mother why it was essential that they should be going aboard their gondola exactly at the minute when Hugh Thurne appeared off their jetty in his, and also why this self-same critically important minute should be the one during which, at the station, the Mancrofts got themselves and their luggage afloat and set off in this direction. Mamma had been on the verge of being perfectly intelligent about all this, and had even annoyed her by mildly disputing the precise time that the Ca' Zante gondola would take to come from there to here. But then the knife-grinder had appeared at the street door, and for some reason her mother had gone down to be talkative and distracted, and to oversee the sharpening of the household's knives, a routine that Elena customarily saw to perfectly well.

Gloria liked the knife-grinder. In the trenches in the Alps he had lost his left foot from frostbite, so these days he swung along through the alleys with his crutch thumping, and his right hand pushing his bicycle, which had been ingeniously adapted to bear a whetstone alongside its front wheel. When it was stationary and firmly propped upright, he mounted it and pedalled furiously, using his good leg as a piston and sparing the other (which had a sort of wooden clog that the doctors had fixed him up with), while he bent forward and held people's knives to his whirring stone in a flurry of sparks and a grating whine.

But now the afternoon was wearing on. Francesco still hadn't come back from the railway station (and since Sergio the gondolier had died, he was the only person who could shift the family so much as a few yards across the water). Gloria knew that it was a total waste of time even to fret about her father's capacity for urgency. And it was more than she could endure to stand in the street while her mother took five minutes to pay the knife-grinder, and then for some reason decided to ask after his parents who still were not old.

Gloria swivelled her feet on the paving, she pouted. The pearly skin on her cheekbones and her forehead went bruise-coloured. She shrugged her thin shoulders when both her mother and the knife-grinder could see her, she flicked her fingers. At last she bolted indoors and up the stairs to her bedroom at the top of the house, knowing that she was in disgrace for her rudeness, but feeling better already thanks to this burst of activity.

Without thinking about it for a second, she resorted to her window, which was her favourite stance in all the world. Passing in a trice from exasperation with her family to utter forgetfulness of them, and then to a consciousness of their existence that was exceedingly hazy but consisted only of admiration and love, she fell to watching the vessels toing and froing below on the Grand Canal, as she had done all her life, ever since she'd been so little that they'd had to lift her up so she could see.

The merit of this vantage-point right now was that Gloria would be able to make out the Ca' Zante boat while it was still way down the Rialto reach, so that she might still be in time to hustle her family afloat with some semblance of punctuality. So to begin with she kept glancing toward the craft to the east, at the same time as she told herself that there was absolutely no point in dashing to a window at the back of the house to peer down and see if that lackadaisical brother of hers was just that moment sauntering home. But then at once the Grand Canal before her and the house at her back came lapping in at her eyes and at her ears as they always did; they settled in her mind with their messages of how life was today, and their memories of how it had been, and their misty thoughts of how it might be going to be.

The house's creaks and its draughts; the light that fell through different windows at different times and seasons; the church bells from near and far, those Grand Canal chimes that had measured out her life; people's voices, caught momentarily from room to room, or echoing in her memory, or coming to her in stories she'd been told; how the house sounded when a gale from the land was roaring, which was different from the sound it made during a sea gale; which trading craft were passing, doing what, at which hour of the day . . . All these would speak to Gloria, as they'd speak to her father, who had been born in that ramshackle old building beside that tideway before her. They'd speak of moods and feelings, though not often in ways she could have translated into utterance.

So now, when the girl propped her elbows on her sill, all the fretfulness left her face. She forgot to keep turning around to her bedside clock to see if everyone was going to be late and her plan would be spoiled. She went off into a dream in which the church of San Stae that stood almost opposite her window, with the weather-stains on its pale bulgy buttresses, took its place in her half-consciousness alongside how the wisps of woodsmoke in the kitchen, which all winter smelled the same as in the other rooms that had fires, somehow had a different nice tang to them when spring came and the other hearths were not lit. The young men who'd lost a leg or an arm in the war, and who now were beggars hunched by the church door over there, which would be all right as a place to linger in today but must have been frightful all winter, took their place beside the stories her father had told her of all the funeral processions that had left the water-gate of this house over the centuries and all the wedding parties that had arrived here. (Gloria had latterly been evading family super-vision more and more successfully; she had discovered kissing; and she was quite sure who the next bride to be rowed back to this house from the church in all her panoply was going to be.) She was just wondering about her great-grandfather, who in the Risorgimento had been one of the leaders of the rebellion against the Austrians and had been killed during the siege, so he'd never seen Venice's second fall, never seen his city retaken, when she focused on Hugh Thurne in his gondola below, who had been approaching for several minutes without her noticing him.

Gloria bounded downstairs, shouting merrily: 'He's here! Come on everybody, all aboard! We're off!'

She ran through the hall, over its uneven and damp paving, between the Ionic columns, a few of which had, over the centuries, lapsed from the immaculately perpendicular, and the walls which long ago had been painted green and pink and white but for decades had been greying dustily. Panting and laughing she reached the water-entrance, flung her hands against the iron trellis-work and gripped it to stop herself slithering.

Nobody had even opened the gate! She heaved at the bolts, she hauled the unwieldy palisade of rusting curlicues back toward her. Stepping gingerly forth onto the seaweedy steps in the sunlight, she exclaimed: 'Here I am! We're coming!'

Instantly she liked Hugh Thurne as much as she always had – and not only because he spoke Italian unlike most foreigners, mixing in a bit of Venetian to amuse himself and her. There he sat in his boat a few feet from her, sensible and unpompous and cheerful, and what he said with a smile was: 'Oh I don't think I need the rest of your family, do I? Hop in with me, Gloria, and we'll be off.'

Just as she had metamorphosed instantaneously from distracted imaginer to hollering tearaway, now at once she was the young lady. 'Oh I don't think, Sir Hugh' – these last two words in English – 'that Mamma would think that was a good idea,' she told him, standing at her canal gate. 'I'm sorry we're late, but I can hear them all coming now. Oh heavens, I haven't got my bonnet!' And she ran back inside to get it.

To Gloria's relief, soon her parents really were getting aboard the family gondola. Even more amazing, Francesco came sauntering down the hall, consulting his new wrist-watch with affected indifference, and giving off a faint aroma of the French cigarette he had smoked in the café a few minutes before. Then suddenly he gave his sister a wink, jumped lithely onto the gunwale, ran aft to the raised stern-deck and picked up his oar.

XIII

'Honestly, I can't imagine why we haven't simply gone to the station to meet Violet!' exclaimed Valentina, arranging her dress over her legs as she took her seat in the faintly rocking hull, and smiling at Hugh to acknowledge the courtesy with which at the sight of her he had raised his trilby a few inches from his head. 'Francesco and Gloria are forever coming up with such fanciful plans. It's astonishing when one in ten of them works as it's meant to.' Then she noticed her son's and her daughter's dancing eyes. They were laughing about something – about her quite possibly, the wretches! She thought of this readiness for delight that they both had, their erupting into joyfulness from one second to the next, which nothing in the world could stop and which, of course, was wonderful in them but could also be inappropriate, and an anxiety struck her.

'My darlings – please – you will remember, won't you? Colonel Mancroft was killed only last September. Particularly when you're with Robert . . . The poor boy won't always feel quite as merry as you do.'

Giacomo Venier remained on his feet in the gondola until his wife was comfortably settled, and then he sat down beside her, agreeably aware that Hugh Thurne and he, without ever having needed to discuss it, were of exactly the same view as to the kind of welcome to Venice they intended to offer Violet Mancroft, and for that matter also as to the Easter holiday that their mutual godson should be given. At the same time he was attempting not to be reminded, as he fatally was whenever he saw Hugh, of how pleasant it must be to be regularly paid the salary appropriate for one of His Britannic Majesty's envoys, rather than to have recently had the inflation in this country obliterate most of the money your family had still had in the bank.

'Hello, old fellow, splendid to see you!' he announced in his rumbling, genial voice. 'You're coming to dinner, aren't you? Haven't forgotten? Excellent! Well, we'll talk when we're ashore. Right you are, Francesco, off we go!' He slapped his hands down on the knees of his old-fashioned suit in order to drive away the thought that today, as on so many days, all he'd done in his office had been to sit there feeling horribly ill and weak, so really he might as well chuck in the pretence of work and never go back. 'Don't worry, Gloria my darling, they're not here yet – I can't even see them ahead. You never know, you may bring off this marvellous meeting of yours.'

None of Giacomo and Valentina Venier's friends were rowed by a son rather than by a paid man, and they still found this novelty rather peculiar. On the one hand, of course it was excellent that, after old Sergio's death, the lad had seized on this method of saving his parents the expense of retaining even a part-time gondolier. On the other hand, his enthusiasm for oarsmanship, for sailing and for generally messing about in boats was a perpetual reminder that he had not as yet manifested any dedication to anything else.

However, these were modern, democratic times, and Giacomo and Valentina were getting accustomed to being seen about town with a member of the family at the oar. Sitting side by side on the tatty seats in their old black craft, they settled down to play their parts good-humouredly in this occasion their son and daughter had organised, and they gazed ahead to see if they could make out a gondola that might be Violet's. After all these years of loving one another, often they were alive to the same tremors of thought at the same time. So now Giacomo took his wife's hand in his. He squeezed it, then for a minute went on holding it: because she was far more alarmed than he was about whatever it was that was wrong with the valves of his heart, because it was rather marvellous that Francesco and Gloria hadn't quite yet finished growing up, and because despite everything here the four of them were.

It had turned into one of those Grand Canal late afternoons when both the water and the sky are mother-of-pearl. The first swifts of the year, flown back from Africa, were towering up above the brown roofs and hurtling down over the water with their screaming calls.

Hugh Thurne had watched his friends getting themselves under way with the satisfaction that family afforded him whatever they did. He was in an even better mood than he had been earlier in the day, having on his way up the Grand

Canal had the double pleasure of deciding what he was going to do, and amusing himself with this inexhaustible ability he appeared to have of being convinced by whatever his latest idea happened to be. In London next week, he'd talk Elizabeth out of getting divorced and remarried. Yes, that was it! He didn't think it would be difficult. If necessary (but he didn't imagine means as unpleasant as these would be called for), he would make it plain to her that he had no intention of doing the gallant thing and letting it appear that all the fault for the failure of their marriage was his. On the contrary, he'd instruct his lawyers to put up the sort of fight that – well, the sort of fight that would make a woman as essentially timid as Elizabeth think twice, make her call the whole kerfuffle off before it came to that. This might be distinctly uncharming behaviour on his part, and it might cause some of his friends to be disappointed in him. But it would be the right thing to do, for family reasons, for all sorts of reasons. Of course, Elizabeth and he would agree to continue to allow each other all the liberty under the sun and the moon. But to go in for second marriages, at their age, and when they'd already demonstrated quite how bad at that particular love relation they both were . . . ! Well, really, that *would* be to overestimate the importance of oneself and of one's feelings quite ridiculously. Flings were appropriate, even a love affair might be passable if conducted self-deprecatingly, but not a marriage. Well, anyhow, that was how matters appeared to him this afternoon, he thought, crossing his legs and smiling to himself and pulling down the brim of his hat the better to watch the swifts.

In the floppy jacket, fulsomely knotted tie and straw hat that these days he and all his friends affected, Francesco had one concern: that the professional gondolier in the Ca' Zante vessel less than a boat's length away should not for a second imagine that he, Francesco, the amateur, was not an equal master of every arcane trick of Venetian oarsmanship, most of which he could perform with one hand in his trouser pocket while also engaging in a conversation. So now he swung his long, heavy oar nonchalantly, without displaying any of his boyish delight in how, when it was poised in its beautifully carved walnut *forcola*, it felt magically light. He glanced astern, narrowing his eyes slightly, as if he was particularly interested in some gulls which had that moment alighted on the water, so it should be perfectly clear that he was not concentrating at all hard on what he was doing. He thought what a bore it was, this banal sculling up and down a short stretch of the Grand Canal, when he'd far rather show how he could manoeuvre his gondola through the narrowest, trappiest catty-corners in town without scratching its paint.

Gloria sat on a stool forrard, her mind visited again for a moment by her great-grandfather Alvise Venier who in 1849 had gone afloat here for the last time, his funeral barge rowed by oarsmen in black breeches and tunics with gold sashes, his coffin covered with the banner of the Lion of Saint Mark. Then she looked across to where tall, thin Hugh Thurne, who always wore that gold watch-chain across his waistcoat, was sitting on his own, and she wished that she'd accepted his invitation to go aboard his boat, because right this minute she'd have been ensconced beside him rather grandly. But now

Sir Hugh was sitting up straighter, he was gazing ahead as if he'd recognised somebody.

Gloria turned to look forward too, suddenly recalling that they were off to welcome real people, who would turn out to be splendid in ways she hadn't foreseen and also be disappointing in ways she hadn't foreseen either. And her Venice, these canals, this lagoon – how would it seem, to the newcomers? She'd never been to Rome, let alone to Paris or to London. What with the war and with her father's ill health, for years she'd hardly ever crossed to the mainland, except in the summers when for a month they all decamped to her cousins' farm in the foothills at Asolo. Would these English think she'd lived rather cooped up? Would they be awed as soon as they entered her world?

Robert Mancroft, who had shed all his wretchedness the instant they had left the railway station and gone aboard their gondola, as if all that was required to achieve freedom of spirit was this deliverance from life on land to life on the lagoon, sat beside his mother as they were borne lilting forward between the churches and the palaces into the soft, scumbled pinks and blues and greys. He had forgotten his father, he had forgotten his old home. He heard her exclaim, 'That's San Geremia!' and then she said something else, but he was far too enchanted to try to remember names. Then he saw two craft coming towards him that suddenly became different from the other water traffic, craft that had an intention in his regard, had a meaning.

Before he had time to work out what was happening, these two vessels started to diverge, to make an opening, as in a fore-ordained movement of a dance. His godfather Hugh waved and called, the people in the other gondola waved and called, his mother was exclaiming gaily to her left and her right – but he didn't hear them. Rapt, he watched the pair of rakish black hulls wheel slowly away from his own on either side, begin to turn in two symmetrical arabesques, and a girl with black wavy hair under a straw bonnet loomed in his sight.

She was gone, the arabesques were nearly completed. But his mother's and his gondolier must have caught the spirit of the dance, because he called something in a smiling voice and he wheeled their boat around, he started an involution, started a lapping and splashing gradual figure-of-eight. And now the other two steersmen were responding each with a second outward turn and arabesque that seemed to Robert to take up most of the width of the Grand Canal.

The girl's pale, beautiful face swung into his vision again. So did her hand on the gunwale. Marvelling, he watched the circling hulls, watched their grace, and the water, and the light.

'Robert's seen a ghost,' came his mother's laughing voice, in which he recognised her anxious love, recognised the dissembling. And then, to him: 'Have I been obtuse, darling, have I missed something?'

'No.'

'Are you all right?'

'Yes. Yes.'

XIV

When the three boats turned for home, Giacomo Venier fell quiet. Valentina's and Hugh's and Violet's cheerful voices echoed in his consciousness; but from far, far off. It was his softened mood this afternoon perhaps; it was seeing Philip's widow and his son certainly; it was a host of other things . . . But suddenly he couldn't bear it, how vulnerable Violet was with that brittle look around her mouth and her eyes, how vulnerable they all were even now that the war was in the past and you could do things like drift around in boats in the sunshine calling out to your friends. For a minute he could not have spoken, for his longing for this spring, this new year of peace, truly to be different from the old years.

Giacomo remembered Hugh's discouraging talk about the political situation in Europe, and about how Marshal Foch, who unfortunately probably *did* know what he was talking about rather more than most other men when it came to this, had muttered that the German question hadn't really been resolved, all they were getting was a truce for twenty years.

107

He remembered the influenza epidemic, which was still killing thousands of people a month all over the Old World, so that to be among the survivors in this first spring after the war didn't mean you were safe. Even his darling Gloria, merrily setting off to school each morning and merrily coming home each afternoon, wasn't safe.

Let the risks be averted, let the influenza epidemic and the other epidemics cease, he prayed, sitting stolidly and silently in his black suit in his black boat with his hands on his knees, his craggy face for a minute looking even more saturnine in repose than it normally did. This of course dreadfully imperfect peace – let it hold, that was the only thing that mattered.

Giacomo Venier had never been a religious man. But he suddenly found that he was giving his neighbours' facades a wistful smile, and he was addressing a prayer of sorts to – oh, to he didn't know what: to the April air, to the approach of evening on the water, to men and their unchanging selfishness, to the life that was still tiredly astir in his own brain. Because you only had to look at valiant, fragile Violet glancing about her brightly to know how desperate, how total was her need to be able to live again after her past. Oh not yet, of course, not yet. But it would be atrocious if she were not to come to life once more before she died; it would be atrocious if, however many more years she walked about on the earth, in essence this was it, this was *finis*. Because you only had to see Gloria with that sparkle in her eyes and those dimples in her cheeks, Gloria who was all amusement, who was all delight, and without those things would be . . .

Well, what would she be? And in the meantime, he thought,

here the seven of them were, bobbing about in their boats on this channel between these houses. Here they were at this hopelessly unstable intersection of their seven lives – but even as soon as next year – what? – who could tell?

Gloria's father frowned; he rubbed the bridge of his nose. Naturally he himself didn't have to be here to see Gloria bonny in years to come, and he wasn't likely to be. He didn't have to be one of those who saw her – what did he mean? – who saw her, not unharmed by life, that was impossible, but with her spirit for the most part intact. But let others see it, he hoped. Let it be there to be seen. Oh and another thing, now that it came to harm. He'd tell Valentina that they could take poor Donatella into the house. One way or another, they'd cope. He could always sell something else.

Then abruptly with a cheerful heave the old man sat straighter in his black seat and his face lit up, because he'd recollected how the other day Gloria had made a tremendous, giggling declaration about how, whether she got married when she wasn't yet twenty or not for a long time, he must promise still to be alive so that he and she could hang onto each other's trembly elbows in the nave of San Marcuola when the day came. In return for which, she absolutely promised that she'd marry a man so rich that he uttered not a murmur about paying for the house to be repaired from its hall to its attic.

Robert was sophisticated enough to know in his bones that he must conceal his fascination with Francesco Venier's sister by at once beginning to make friends with that young man. This for the moment was impossible, because Francesco was

109

standing in command on the raised stern of one gondola, while he himself was sitting, an ignominious passenger no better than a piece of luggage, in another. It was not even possible to ignore Gloria, because their boats were gunwale to gunwale as they headed toward her house. Mercifully everyone else was talking, so that with luck nobody would notice if he and she were a bit tongue-tied at first. Even so, he was close enough to see the faint dusting of freckles on the creamy skin of her cheeks. He could nearly have reached to touch the soft curve of her chin, and he caught the black glisten in her eyes when she gave him a slow, sly look.

No, she had done nothing of the kind! He *must* have imagined that! And now yet again he was gazing at the side of her head she was presenting to him; he was breaking all his resolves to be simply a guest who was delighted to have arrived.

Robert twisted jerkily in his seat, because he'd just remembered how people would tease him if they suspected anything. Either that, or they'd ignore and despise him. *She* would despise him, she'd instantly exploit any weakness he showed. Yes – but that slow dance of black hulls, that air's pale shimmer on the tide's gleaming . . . Oh God, he must think of something else quickly, because otherwise quite soon she'd say something to him, and the second she did that he'd go as red as a beetroot, he just knew he would. The curve of a high stern that swung slowly away, the arc made by an oar . . . Already it was fading.

When Francesco reached home he brought his gondola alongside its two mooring-posts. (They were painted white and blue, with ornate golden tops in the shape of turbans, like the ornamental knots that sailors called Turks' heads.) The second vessel could then come alongside the first and the third alongside the second.

Everybody stood up in the wobbling hulls. There was a light knocking of gunwales, a clatter as Francesco shipped his oar. Voices rose in a low hubbub: 'Hang on a second, I haven't yet made fast.' 'Well, here we are!' 'No, nothing has changed. No improvements at all . . .'

Gloria was the first to swing herself up onto the jetty. Giacomo, who was still surprisingly steady on his feet in a boat, offered Violet his arm so she could step from her gondola to his, and stood beaming as the two ladies embraced. Then very gallantly and gracefully he took Violet's elbows, smiling into her eyes and drawing her toward him so he could kiss her on both cheeks. 'Welcome!' he said. 'Welcome!' Francesco busied himself with his mooring warps, without glancing around at the other two oarsmen, before he jumped up onto the planks of the jetty. Then he stood ready to shake the visitors' hands and to carry their suitcases indoors.

Hugh Thurne too was on his feet. But he let all the others do their disembarking before him, while he enjoyed the sight of this dilapidated house (it had not been replastered since the eighteenth century and a lot of the brickwork was exposed), which had kept the weather off hundreds of years of babies being born and people of all ages dying, these tide-sluiced steps where men and women with all manner of intentions in their hearts had arrived, and news had arrived that had occasioned mourning or rejoicing. He thought how nice a change it would be to stay for a while in a house such as this one which faced south, rather than at Ca' Zante which faced north and had never needed blinds, though it did offer the daily spectacle of the sunlight on the palaces opposite, which the Veniers never had. He thought what a good frieze of figures the welcomers and the welcomed on the jetty before his eyes made against the foot of the discoloured facade. Then he began stepping toward them from boat to boat with his long legs, taking off his hat as he came.

'Now I can give you a *real* hug!' Valentina Venier exclaimed, with tears in her happy voice as the two women embraced for the second time.

'Heavens, after all these years . . .!' Violet Mancroft murmured, glancing up at the windows above her head.

The master of the house now gave all his attention to Robert, shaking his hand vigorously and using his other arm to give the boy's shoulder a terrific squeeze. 'I haven't a clue whether you'll find any English that Francesco or Gloria may speak in your hearing comprehensible, but don't worry about that, you'll pick up some Italian in no time. Anyhow, the three of you will discover you can get along in French, I imagine – you're all *meant* to be learning it. Now . . . Your other godfather tells me you shoot well. Not yet as formidably as your father shot – I wasn't expecting that – but well. Of course, you've come at the wrong time of the year – but might Christmas be possible? We ought to be able to offer you some wildfowling. Do you know, one evening the winter you were born, your father and I each shot a right and left

112

of teal on the river at Brack. But the trouble was, ten minutes later he did it again, and I haven't done it since.'

Hugh waited until the more imperative embracings had been concluded and then he turned to Violet.

'Oh yes, I suppose I'm longing to kiss you, you old reprobate,' she said, raising her eyebrows to Valentina in mock despair and then dabbing her mouth against Hugh's jaw. 'Upward of half a year, and . . . Oh yes, I know you wrote, and I believe that eventually I even replied. But you haven't come to see me – since – since he . . . Well, you haven't come tramping in through the door, Hugh, have you, either in the country or in London? Busy, yes, you don't have to say it. Busy! A war to fight and then a peace to fight. Men's stuff.' Her voice light, distanced. 'Paris to look after, Venice to look after, your family to overlook.' For a second, her eyes met his. 'Tomorrow, your house, after dinner?'

The ladies moved off the jetty and in through the *pietra d'Istria* archway. Giacomo Venier and Hugh Thurne hesitated, each giving the other an enquiring, affectionate, quizzical glance that said approximately: 'Are you all right? You don't look too bad. Well, now everybody else has been taken care of, we can concentrate on each other for a minute. Excellent!' Then they grinned, clapped one another on the shoulder and went indoors.

'This work that's started on the new port at Marghera, and on what looks like being a whole modern town on the mainland,' Hugh began at once, 'the trouble will be the politicians, eh? Some of these Nationalists are a bit shrill for my liking. Of course Foscari has been pushing the Marghera project for years – but Count Volpi is more powerful now, wouldn't you say?'

'All this land reclamation, all these ugly new buildings, all this dredging,' Giacomo grumbled equably as they reached the pilasters at the foot of the staircase. 'I've shot duck along those shores every winter since I was a boy, but now . . . I was just saying to our godson that I'd try to fix him up with some mallard flighting at Christmas, but it'll have to be in the northern lagoon. Now, come up and let's have a drink.'

Robert Mancroft had been completely disarmed by his host's welcome, so that he was already nearly as in love with all Gloria's family as he was with her. He had merrily heaved suitcases from boat to boat and up to Francesco on the jetty, and now he found the right thing to ask him straight away.

'Rowing a gondola,' he began gingerly, with an apologetic smile for using his own language. 'I dare say it's fiendishly difficult, but is there any chance you might let me have a go one day? Would you show me how it's done? I can sail, I'm not a complete idiot in a boat.'

'*Dio mio*, fiendishly? *Che cosa vuol' dire, questo* fiend?' But then, 'Yes, yes, of course,' Francesco hastened on with hospitable courtesy. 'Difficult . . . ? Is not so difficult as speak English. I learn in one summer, to row.'

'You must learn Italian,' Gloria told Robert in that language, suddenly appearing beside him and holding out her hand. 'Or . . . *Parles-tu français? Tous les anglais parlent un peu de français, n'est-ce pas?*' Then without waiting for him to reply, she asked her brother: 'Rowing? Well, at least there's the possibility that he might fall in. And he'd get frightful blisters on his hands at first, that would be all right. You could teach me too, after all your empty promises. He and I could get blisters and fall in together. Only probably I wouldn't fall in. We could fetch out the old *sandolo* that's been mouldering in there for years.' She swung back to Robert and said in her hesitant, schoolroom English, 'Come and see.'

'Called a *sandolo*,' Gloria told him, pointing to a shabby skiff that lay upturned on trestles in one of the shadowy aisles beyond the columns. 'Smaller than a gondola. If you like boats, if you like the sea.' She was standing close beside him, and they were still near enough to the water-gate to be in the part of the hall where the last of the day's sunshine reflected off the Grand Canal wavered over the stonework and over her. Her eyes met his. 'We could go out into the lagoon. If you're interested.' Then she tossed over her shoulder to her brother: 'Needs a lick of paint, the poor old boat, but then it'll be all right.'

XV

Oh, I still think this wretched country of mine could have stayed neutral perfectly well, like Holland, like Spain. Why not?

Robert was exhausted and he had been lying in his bed for a quarter of an hour at least, but the men's voices from dinner were still echoing in his head.

And what sticks in my gullet, Hugh, when I think of the casualties on both sides, when I think of the destruction, is that all through that spring of '15 our government was still trying to get a better price in territory for entering the war on Austria's side than they got out of the French and out of you English, at least on paper. So what happened? A child could have predicted it! Giacomo Venier had flourished his already slightly fish-stained napkin, had given his lips a further wipe, had sipped his wine. *In early May the Austrians finally got around to offering us the bait of the Trentino, which before they'd refused so much as to discuss – and which since it's a province where*

117

most of the people speak Italian was one of the few good reasons for a quarrel that we had. The trouble was, in late April we'd already signed that secret Treaty of London with you – though in our duplicitous fashion we still hadn't got around to denouncing the Triple Alliance that for donkey's years had tied us up in a bundle with Germany and Austria. So at the end of May we had to go to war against the Austrians anyway, despite their having offered us the main thing that we wanted. What do you reckon about England? Looking back now . . . Could you have stayed out of the war, or was it inevitable?

Oh – Lord . . . Well – it was inevitable once Germany had decided to attack in the west. Lying on his back with his hands behind his head and gazing up happily into the dimness (he'd left his curtains open in order not to be deprived of the starlight), Robert recalled how his English godfather had taken off his spectacles and weighed them for a moment in his hand. *For centuries, in those British Isles of ours, if we've wanted to stay free we've been compelled to have a policy of backing up any secondary European powers that were prepared to stand up for themselves and fight whichever tyranny it was that happened to be attempting to dominate the continent at the time. In the case of this latest threat . . . Well, in '14 we only had to imagine the danger to us of a defeated France that became a vassal state of Germany. Then Denmark and Holland and Belgium, even if any of them had been left with some nominal independence, would have been Germany's for the picking, and certainly they'd have been of no conceiv-*

able defensive use to us. No, these days the North Sea and the Channel are only a last ditch. With modern warfare what it is, the line that's got to be held so far as we're concerned is the Rhine.

Robert wriggled luxuriously beneath his sheets and blankets, his tired mind aswim with how at dinner their elders had assumed that Francesco and he and even Gloria would not be too ill informed and would have opinions. He remembered how delicious the tureen of mussels had smelled when it was borne to the table, and how Gloria, instead of passing him the bread rolls, had glanced mischievously around, snatched one up and pitched it at his head. He remembered how his hostess had talked to him about his father in the most natural way, not avoiding the subject but not being upsetting either, so that now, lying snugly in bed in her house, it seemed to him that Valentina Venier and he had in some mysterious way been friends for years. Then he listened again, he heard his Venetian godfather chuckling as he began a story.

The other day I was walking past the Scalzi, which they're only now beginning to repair, when I bumped into that roly-poly man – I'll remember his name in a minute. He made a heap of money, he bought himself a title, he married a pretty woman called Tiziana Something-or-other. You must have met him, Hugh. Come to think of it, I believe his business has been in mortars and machine-guns, so why he should have been so outraged by a spot of war damage I'm not sure. He's never shown any interest in churches or in paintings before. Anyhow, he started

inveighing most righteously to me about how awful it was
that an Austrian airman had dropped a bomb on the Scalzi
where the ceiling had been by Giambattista Tiepolo –
despite it's being fairly obvious that the fellow was trying
to aim his bomb at the railway station next door, so it
was a case of a near miss. I got fed up with this anti-
Austrian rant of his, so I told him we Italians only had
ourselves to blame if our towns and villages all over the
north-east had been shelled for three years, and if a beau-
tiful painting here was in smithereens, because we'd
declared war on Austria-Hungary, not them on us this
time, so of course they'd had to fight. Heavens, he was
angry! He drew himself up to his full height – not very
high in his case. 'Good God, Venier! I'd have expected a
bit more patriotism than that!'

Violet Mancroft had been given the loveliest of the spare
bedrooms, with its four-poster, with its paintings of saints
and of naval battles and of carnivals, with its vast porcelain
stove that had come from the Tyrol. Robert was in the small
dressing-room next door, but he too had a window over the
Grand Canal. For a few minutes after he had lain down he'd
heard his mother moving about, but then her bed-springs
creaked. 'Good night!' he called, though they had already
said good night, and her gentle voice answered, 'Sleep well,
my darling.' But by now half an hour at least must have
passed since then, and he still seemed to be unutterably weary
and at the same time wide awake. He thought how perfectly
right it was, the way this family lived here with the sea
lapping at their front door. Then a nervous tenseness started

to knot itself in Robert's stomach and in his mind, so he knew he wasn't going to escape to sleep so freely as all that. He yanked aside the bedclothes and went to sit on the window-seat in his pyjamas.

He had at once liked Francesco immensely, but there was the horrible awareness that he'd set out to make a friend of him for reasons that weren't quite what they should be, so Francesco might be a splendid fellow but he himself wasn't. Right from the outset, things had wrongness in them! and it was he who introduced it.

That was one miserable succession of ideas.

The other was his excited, humiliating need to know whether there really had been a sly flicker in Gloria's eyes when she looked at him, whether she was as seduced by the dream of pleasure as he was. (This dream was not in much focus, but it was overwhelming.) And when she'd stood between the columns, with the sunlight off the water trembling across her – when the blood had cascaded in his head – when he'd known he *had* to touch her, and he'd known this was impossible, he would never be capable of it . . . That wasn't enchantment. That was being enslaved, and it was appalling to love it.

Why, why had everything within him and around him become difficult and wretched since his father died? ('Since Daddy died' was how he habitually thought of his torments, although in these same years of his late boyhood, alongside bereavement and exile, after long germination and hesitant buddings had come the double florescence of desire and ratio-cination.) And was it going to end, in time? Would things ever get simpler and happier, or was the rest of his life all going to be like this?

In a despairing convulsion, Robert hunched up with his face rammed against his knees, but after a few seconds the agonies in his mind were still there. Making himself sit normally and look out of the window, he set himself to reason about what bedevilled him just as he had tried to do earlier in the day in the train, this time without much expectation that it would do any good, but knowing in his lonely way that he didn't have any other manner of coming to his own assistance. And just then, over the roofs away at Rialto, a brilliant cusp showed.

He caught his breath, his face was utterly calm. How quickly the moon came up! Already it was rising past the chimneys, it was making the whole night sky more silvery than before. The Grand Canal was glittering like – like . . . Oh, he didn't know what like – but Francesco was all right, Francesco had it pretty lucky, Robert thought distractedly, completely forgetting about how he'd wanted to reason his way forward from A to B to C, and instead effortlessly beginning to perceive a few things plainly.

Francesco's father hadn't been killed, his sister hadn't died when she wasn't yet one and a half, he hadn't been chucked out of his home. He hadn't even been sent to some cretinous boarding-school hundreds of miles away in a part of the country that would never mean anything to him. Here he and Gloria were, with their father at one end of the table and their mother at the other. Here they were, with their stories about funny things that had happened, with their plans about how tomorrow morning they were going to take him out in the gondola. While he . . .

Without having consciously come to any conclusion at all, and without feeling either happy or unhappy, Robert suddenly understood what had often seemed to him his irrevocable bad luck, and the sense of desolation that appeared to get itself caused by one thing one day and by another the next but that never failed to find him out. How chancy life was! And how out of your control! That was at the root of it. You happened to be the child of a second marriage. Your sister died when you were so young that honestly you didn't know if you remembered her or not – whether it was just stories, and the photographs of a baby girl that your mother took with her everywhere. Your father was one of the men who didn't come home from the war . . . What richness or joy could there ever be in the consequences of any of this? – all of it so lacking in intelligent purpose, none of it possible for you either to alter or to escape from.

Well, he thought, so that's it! Even so, I'd better get back into bed.

XVI

Robert fell asleep peacefully, but when he woke up in daylight his mother was sitting on the side of his bed with her anxious love in her eyes.

'You cried out. You kept crying out something. Oh my poor boy, it isn't easy for you. I know, I know.'

In dread of the effect that self-pity could have on him, Robert scrambled out of bed without looking at her and started splashing cold water on his face. 'We're going out on the lagoon this morning. I'm hungry. What do people have for breakfast in Venice?'

Gloria had not dared to invite her mother's teasing by putting on anything more fetching than an everyday blue dress, slightly faded after repeated launderings, which she'd often worn when going out for days on the water with her brother. She had, however, allowed herself a tortoiseshell comb in her hair. And she'd slipped on her favourite bracelet of gold and coral which she'd never before subjected to the risks of a day's boating.

Her head and her right wrist thus discreetly enhanced, and her black eyes at least as joyous as they habitually were on sunshiny mornings in the holidays, she had gone out early with her father, as the two of them did every day without fail, if necessary even battling through cloudbursts with boots and umbrellas, to the *pasticceria* at the Anconeta, which in their opinion was the finest in the neighbourhood for pastries and tarts and sweetmeats of all kinds. Here their ritual never varied. The father would buy his copy of the *Corriere della Sera*, and then stand for a minute in the little square, among the cats and the awnings and the people sauntering to work, frowning at the front page of his paper and formulating wry dismissals of the country's politicians. Meanwhile the daughter would buy *brioches* to carry home for everybody's breakfast, after much deliberation choosing those with marmalade, or those with honey, or the plain ones, or a combination of all three. Then with the *Corriere* refolded and a plentiful supply of pastries stowed in a paper bag, the two of them would drink their first cup of coffee of the day, standing companionably at the café door.

This morning Gloria when she was at home again amused herself by dumping a third *brioche* on Robert's plate while he was still munching his second, and by continually filling up his cup with scalding coffee and milk. Then she hurtled downstairs ahead of him. She jumped on board the gondola and started to heave the green cover off its seats, while he stood awkwardly on the jetty above her. She folded the canvas in a clumsy roll and lifted it up to him so their eyes met and their hands touched.

All around her, Gloria could feel the effervescence of the spring morning. It went well with the tingle in the air that there'd been between Robert and her yesterday and there was again now. It went well too with her absolute confidence that she would (in unexamined, infallible ways) know how to manage this tingle in whatever fashion she chose, know how to delight in it and make nothing of it.

She enjoyed being the local girl who knew about these Venetian vessels and their moorings and their equipment, while her guest – for whom according to her parents she ought to have been doing everything possible to make feel at home – had to watch attentively and listen unconfidently. She enjoyed the motions of her arms and legs in his sight. Boys only a couple of years older than her had never yet been at all interesting or attractive – her experiments in flirtation and in cuddling had so far been conducted with a university friend or two of her brother's, and even with one young man so venerable that she had attended his twenty-first birthday celebrations and had lied to him about her age. But now her spirit had been primed by her parents' stories about the Mancrofts, Robert's father's death had given him a sadness and a strange glamour that had got into her blood; and she was determined in her cloudy way that now he'd come flitting across France to her she was going to astound him with her labyrinth of canals, her churches and palaces, her islands in the lagoon.

Mercifully it was only half conscious, but it was unerring, Gloria's instinct for delight and for power, her instinct to overwhelm Robert with this Venice she'd been born to –

because however intensely he gloried in it, she'd all her life glory in it more deeply and more intimately, because however much she offered, there'd always be more that she withheld. She had even already begun to construct vague plans about how, if he came back to Italy in the summer, when it was sweltering and fetid down here in the lagoon, he could join them up at La Badia, her cousins' place near Asolo. Up there in the foothills of the Dolomites there were strawberries, there were figs, there were melons. Robert and she would gallop the horses, they'd swim in the river pools. When they came back to the villa in the evening, they'd see the gigantic old mulberry trees mirrored stirring in its upper windows, thick and green, breeze-ruffled, darted through by hungry finches and buntings.

In the lapping quietness and the April sun, all was peace. The Grand Canal sent ripples of reflected light steadily ascending the facade. In the distance, a thick spout of blackish smoke showed where one of the new steam ferries was passing the market, but here it was so still that when a firewood barge was rowed by they could hear the creak of the oars. The men had long strips of blue and red cotton bound around their heads to keep the sweat out of their eyes.

The clatter of a window being shoved open above Gloria's head made her gaze up.

'Papa!' she shrilled. 'Don't chuck your cigar down on my hair like you did that time! Remember?'

Valentina Venier, standing arm in arm with Violet Mancroft at the water-gate to watch the young people set off for their day on the water, had lain awake until three in the morning in order to arrive at the unproblematic conclusion that her dinner party had not been hopelessly unsuccessful. Now she was feeling responsible because Violet and she were going to be alone together for much of the day, and anxious because long discussion – perilous, irresistible – was impending. Also, Hugh Thurne's presence last night had agitated her with its usual muddle of the wish to make much of him, the wish to condemn him, the wish to love him, and the wish never to have him cross her threshold or her mind again. And Violet was going to see him after dinner – and they'd have a lot to talk about, those two, that they wouldn't dream of sharing with Giacomo and her. Indeed, one of the reasons why Violet had accepted her invitation, why she'd brought that nice tousle-headed son of hers here for his Easter holiday, was no doubt Hugh's having become a sort of part-time Venetian. And he was involved in yet another disreputable liaison, apparently – that was the tittle-tattle.

'Francesco, whatever you do you *must* bring them back in time for lunch!' his mother burst out with a vehement primness quite uncharacteristic of her, giving Violet's elbow an affectionate squeeze and then frowning unhappily because she could not but notice when this friendly pressure of her arm was not returned. (Violet was screwing up her eyes against the sun and gazing off down the tideway, remembering.)

'In time for lunch?' Francesco sounded surprised, but not interested enough to be irritated. 'Oh I don't know, Mamma . . . We may buy a picnic like we often do and not be home till evening.' He gave his sister a quick grin, and with a couple of nonchalant reverse strokes of his oar he glided his boat clear of the jetty. 'Or we may go to a restaurant – or we could if any of us had any money. Perhaps Robert's pockets are bulging with the stuff. Or hang on, I know . . . We'll get the restaurant to send the bill to Papa.'

'What did I tell you about them?' Trying more consciously now to distract herself from the undercurrent of her thoughts, Valentina gave a determined puff of laughter. 'Truly I could hope that boat of theirs springs a leak a fair distance from the nearest island – that might damp them down a little! Now darling, we've got hours to ourselves, with a spot of luck. What shall we do? I mean, apart from beginning to tell one another about these terrible years. That bitter winter when Philip and you were here for the last time . . . Even by day the north winds seemed to be black – I've been remembering it in such detail! The blizzards of sleet, the roaring fires we lit, the hot punches that Giacomo and Philip kept concocting – everything! But now . . . What would *you* like to do? Shall we loll in the drawing-room, or would you rather stroll somewhere? A new bookshop has opened at San Grisostomo. Giacomo says we must patronise it with wild extravagance or they'll go bust. Oh Lord, I . . .' This time, Valentina's distractedness was involuntary, and caused by her mother's instinct, which had already picked up the beginnings of a beguilement between Gloria and Robert. She *hoped* Violet was going to be as amused and charmed by this as she herself would be. Even more, she hoped that Giacomo was going to be sensible and cheerful when Gloria started to have crushes, or rather when they became such that even he, besotted with the girl as he'd always been, couldn't fail to notice them.

As Robert stepped aboard, Gloria sketched him a roguish curtsy. 'Now we shall sit here,' she began in French, and continued in English, 'like a lady and a lord.' Then in Italian to her brother, airily: 'Right, my good man, let's be off. The canal up past the Maddalena, please, and then out to the lagoon.'

The lady and the lord sat side by side in their black seats, delectably conscious of one another, and, with language being so defective a means of communication, very contented not to say much, but to enjoy other interchanges, which were more eloquent.

They had hardly entered the Maddalena canal when a swarm of bees on the wall of a house caused a commotion of neighbours leaning out to close their windows with a bang, especially when the seething hummock of insects began to shed buzzing patrols and looked like swarming once more. Francesco and Robert grinned. Gloria laughed with delight. 'They'll have come from the Servi nunnery garden,' she decided, 'those are the nearest hives to here. Just look at that fat woman, she's so frightened she's getting furious with the catch of her window.' But then their vessel glided on, and already the promise of the lagoon she loved started to possess her.

Tens of thousands of hectares of inland sea; littoral fishing villages and island villages; islands that were woods and ruins and swamps; marshes of sea lavender and samphire where you sculled along creeks, only the reed-cutters and you disturbing the curlew and the egret . . . All this was Gloria's birthright, it had been Francesco's and hers since they had

131

been so young they'd played with their toys on the boat's floorboards, while old Sergio had rowed steadily along, and Papa and Mamma had enjoyed the slow clouds overhead and had presided over the lunch hamper. Those inlets rimmed with tamarisk trees where beached wherries rotted; a church tower shimmering far off across miles of water; marshmen's dykes and sluices and jetties; the fish-pens and the brackish hayfields; the quietness . . . All were a peace and a freedom that Gloria had always known and that she had need of. So now she pondered how to ask Robert in French or in English something along the lines of, 'Do you like tumbledown remains of island fortresses all overgrown with brambles and nettles?' but it was too difficult and anyway she lost interest in saying it.

This morning Robert still had a disheartening sense of inferiority to Francesco, who had so much that he didn't have, and who was so much at home standing on his high stern with his oar in his hands. But by the time the gondola was slipping out between the last flanking houses, he was half beguiled by the reflected facades, by the birdsong from behind garden walls, by the comedy of the bees. And now here was a busy wharf. Blue immensities stretched before him and promised islands. He was back in a world that he seemed to recognise, so he sat up straight and glanced delightedly around.

A coasting collier was moored at the quay. Blackened men trudged up and down her grimy gangplanks, a derrick was being swung. Farther along, two schooners lay, their sails furled along their gaffs, which were etched high and dark against the dazzle of the sun.

Francesco began to row clear of the quay, heading off vaguely in the direction of an island called Le Vignole, he said, and the hubbub of seamen, merchants, ships' chandlers, and women with stalls or baskets was already dying in Robert's ears. There lay the graveyard island with its cypresses greenish-black against the radiance, which in a few minutes they'd be leaving to port. Far away to starboard, he could see taller derricks, and a destroyer anchored in the tideway. That was the Arsenale down there, Gloria said. And right here, becalmed before his happy eyes, was a majestic barge with her tan sails hanging motionless. Yes, but where had he lived something very like this? What was stealing back to him, and from when?

The collier unloading and the trading schooners were just like English east-coast ports he knew, where before the war his father had taken him to see the wharves and the ships. In one of those estuary towns – but which one? – there'd been a story about an old harbour-master who at low tide would lean his elbow on his cutter's cockpit with a 2.2 rifle and shoot the rats running over the mud slopes. Yes, yes, but it wasn't that . . . Some other memory was there, still hidden in the murk in his brain – but what was it? He must concentrate. No, the trick was not to concentrate, but to let it come of its own free will. This vast blue stillness, and church towers far off, and a tern that dived . . .?

Francesco was rowing past the barge, they were already at her slack foresails. Now her towering mainsail and topsail had come between the azure sky and them, they were in shade and Robert remembered. His father and he had been sailing the half-decker *Calypso*. It had been a glassy day, for a while they'd been becalmed a mile or so off the coast with its russet-roofed villages and its flint church towers. Daddy had let him idle the time away by taking the little scow for a row.

The varnished scow called *Tiddler*, and he a boy of maybe twelve. *Calypso*'s elegant hull and her bowsprit, her tapering mast and gaff, her foresails and mainsail and topsail poised in the sea glitter. Then as now, a smaller craft inching past a greater one had lost the sunshine behind tall sails. There as here, far off, mediaeval towers.

Robert gazed up at the barge's shroud of canvas that now had sunlight beginning to sparkle along its rope-lined leech because the gondola was moving all the time, soon the moment would pass. He turned to Gloria beside him, as if to say something.

XVII

'Keep going on up, Violet, we're not there yet. I mean – of course you can have this storey if you'd rather. You must pitch your camp in any bit of the house you fancy. But I had thought you might feel more independent and peaceful higher up. What's more, if you go for the top floor you get the loggia, which is about the nicest place in the world to drink a glass of wine on a summer evening. I say,' Hugh Thurne allowed himself to burst out cheerfully, 'I can't help thinking this is rather a brilliant idea I've had! Of course London doesn't particularly appeal to you right now – and here this place is, practically empty. How long are the Veniers expecting you to stay with them? Well, it'll give me time to have these rooms spring-cleaned for you and smartened up a bit. Hang on, I'm going to see if I can turn on a light or two. The whole house has been fitted up with electric light – very modern. The only thing we *haven't* got up here is anything much in the way of heating, but I'll get hold of some stoves between now and the autumn. Would a few paraffin stoves be all right?'

Violet Mancroft had reached the head of the marble stair-case. In the glimmer of the weak electric light, she was running her finger-tips over the reliefs on a pilaster.

'Heavens, Hugh, this is quite a house! Do you know, ten-odd years ago when darling Giacomo and Valentina decided they were going to have electricity, they only got around to having it installed in the ground floor and the first floor. Up above that, where I don't suppose you ever go, in the upper *sala* that's never used and in the bedrooms where they've put Robbie and me, and higher up again where the children live, it's still wonderfully dark and romantic, we go around with brass lamps in our hands. I'm sorry, what did you say? Oh yes, there must be an ironmonger around the corner who'll sell us a couple of stoves. But honestly, I don't think I can accept all this from you. Venice is only an idea, I haven't made up my mind about anything. And I certainly don't need three bedrooms!' she protested, following him doubtfully as he went ahead shoving open doors.

'I should think you might easily. One each for Robert and you, one for visitors. The loggia is through there, on the south side. And here . . . Oh Lord, here the light *doesn't* come on. Just a minute, I'll switch on the lamp on the writing-table, yesterday it was working all right. So . . . This is the library, which would be your sitting-room. I only ever come up here to write letters and I can easily shift my paper and envelopes to one of the desks downstairs.'

More struck every minute by what good spirits Hugh was in as he strode about doing all this showing and all this offering, and her heart tense with what a fine, dear friend of

Philip's and hers he'd been for so many years, Violet stood looking at him, her two top front teeth just visible as she bit her lower lip in a way she'd always had when she was thinking and she was beginning to be amused. She tapped one high-heeled foot on the rug, cocked her head a little to one side.

'A drawing-room beneath our feet, and an even finer one below it on the first floor – not to mention all the other rooms that over the centuries must have been offices, bedrooms, studies, boudoirs, whatever people needed. Yes, I imagine you can probably find a corner somewhere to write your letters.'

'I know!' He grinned. 'Scandalous, isn't it? – but I love it! Well . . . As you're aware, thanks to Elizabeth's father and indeed thanks also to her grandfather, she's never needed to concern herself with my paltry earnings, so I'm free to spend my salary as I please. And this place has been . . . It's been a way of being detached and alone occasionally, and a way of trying to begin to be myself again. Of course, if Venice hadn't been politically and commercially ruined these last hundred years, I'd never have been able to afford it. And I can't help hoping that now . . . Oh, I hope that for you in this sad, sad time – if you want to be a little detached – if you want to be left in peace to start to wonder who what's left of you is, to wonder who she might wish to be in time to come . . . Well, anyhow, here this set-up is, Violet, if you think you might have a use for it. You'd be totally private up on this floor. For that matter, seeing as how I'm here so infrequently, for a lot of the year you'd have the whole house to yourself, not just this apartment.'

'I'd have to pay you rent, Hugh.'

He stood frowning at her smilingly. 'Dear God, it's good to see you again, despite your silly remarks like that last one. Violet, there's so much I want to ask you about Philip! You know, I hadn't seen him since before the war. We'd written, of course, once in a while, telling each other how much we were looking forward to getting back to our old way of life as soon as the fighting was over. But for four years we'd each of us been in a fine variety of countries, including England now and then, but never in the same country at the same time. There's so much I want to remember with you, when you think you can face it, and so much I want to know about how you've been since his death and how you are now. Sometimes, perhaps, when you feel like it, you'll come downstairs and find me and we'll talk, or you'll invite me up here. By the way – it's all right to ask you, isn't it? Philip left Robert and you decently provided for? He must have done. So, what do you think of this place? Might it suit you?' Suddenly unsettled by how happy he'd been made simply by talking to her, he broke off, wondering about that and completely forgetting the questions he'd asked. What good friends they'd been, ever since she first met Philip! How right it felt that she was here, in this shadowy room with its armchairs and its books! Her high cheekbones and the tilt of her nose, that head of chestnut hair – without his knowing whether he was seeing more or remembering more, Hugh's eyes and his mind's eye drank her in.

'Robbie and I had hardly seen Philip during the war either – just for a few short leaves,' Violet began hesitantly, meeting his gaze with a surprised, questioning look and then turning away from it. 'When he was killed, he hadn't been at home for two and a half years. It's worse for Robbie than for me. He was thirteen when his father really went out of his life. Then for four years, all the time he was growing up, he was left with that cruel, cruel hope.'

Violet opened one of the windows and stood jerkily fumbling a cigarette into her silver holder, gazing out at the moonlight reflected in the windows of the palaces opposite. Then she glanced vertiginously down to the Ca' Zante gondola moored below her at the foot of the facade, the boat that had just brought her from the Venier house and in an hour or two would take her back. Because although she was in the grip of how right it felt to be alone with Hugh Thurne at last, to be alone with him to face all that they had lived and all that over time they were going to want to remember and to wonder about, she was also already nervously longing to get away from him. She was looking forward to being alone for her midnight dawdle back up the Grand Canal to a house of less troubling presences.

'Here, let me hold a match to that cigarette for you. Now, what about a nightcap? You'll keep me company, won't you?'

'Mmnn, please.' Violet exhaled the smoke of her cigarette gratefully. With a wistful smile, she watched Hugh go lounging lankily across the room to a small table that held decanters and glasses, just as she'd seen him do so often in rooms in England when Philip had been alive. Then she thought, Ah, so he doesn't only write letters up in this library at the top of the house. It's also where he sometimes has a drink late at night, and no doubt I'm far from being the first person who's been invited to join him here.

The singer that she'd heard Hugh was entangled with these days; how before the war Philip and she had taken an amused interest in their friend's misdemeanours; her not having yet lit upon any trace of a feminine presence in this house . . . All this tumbled through Violet's head as she stood looking at him, her right elbow cradled in her left palm and her cigarette in the fingers of her right hand, her head cocked to one side a little, her teeth once more catching her lower lip. She reminded herself that Hugh's susceptibilities were no more of her business now, except as a source of amusement, than they'd been in the past. She decided that all the same she didn't think she was going to accept his offer of this flat if it would mean her *continually* bumping into his gorgeous, worldly creatures on the staircase. She suppressed an instant's vanity and petulance, during which she'd been about to flaunt her slow way across the rugs and remind him who she was, and said: 'By the way, Elizabeth may not like you, but I bet she likes your knighthood.'

Violet leaned against one of the columns of the windows, so she could feel how cool the marble was between her shoulder-blades. She tossed her chin up, with a gesture that started by being one of pride, but was also a shaking herself free of thoughts she didn't need, and ended by being a motion of weariness as she laid her head against the stone.

'Money, Hugh?' she remembered vaguely. 'Oh, we're going to be all right. Not rich in any conceivable sense of the word, but all right.' She shoved the column away with her back. 'Or at least we'll be all right so long as sterling goes on being worth roughly what it's worth now, and so long as the stock

market doesn't indulge in too many antics of the disappointing sort. Pensioned off, we've been – modestly but
adequately pensioned off. And of course I'd known all along
that, if Philip was killed, Robbie's and my life weren't going
to be anything like as – what? – as splendid as they had been
at Brack.'

Violet had smoked most of her cigarette and tossed it out
of the window; she was fretting back and forth across the
room before Hugh's frowning, compassionate eyes.

'That the estate and the investments and everything would
go to Philip's first son . . . primogeniture – it's terribly important in a lot of primitive societies. That he deliberately hadn't
left Robbie, oh, I don't know, one of the farmhouses or something . . . I knew all this. That Philip didn't *want* Robbie
hanging around his half-brother's estate for the rest of his
days, that he knew how bright he is, he believed in him, he
knew he . . . Oh God, Hugh, I'm sorry. No, don't worry. I'm
not going to break down, you don't need to be afraid of that.
Well, Robbie was always the apple of his father's eye, none
of the rest of us was ever left in much doubt about that. As
for me . . . I've been strong. I've been weak. I've been strong
again and weak again. And it's more than half a year now.
Though if you'd been around when the news came, you'd
have been the person I . . . But you weren't around, were you?
So . . . Well, here I am. Alive, wouldn't you say? For heaven's
sake, Hugh, sit down! Just because I'm not very good at being
still or being poised or whatever it is – just because nights
come when there's a turmoil and misery in me that – I don't
know. But forget your manners, can't you, please, and sit

141

down! You look awkward, which is all wrong for you. Anyway, you're too tall!'

Hugh sat down as instructed, his heart thumping with how thin she was and how beautiful as she twisted and turned before him in the dimness of the one lamp among the bookcases, and his heart thumping too with how he must be a strength to her and to her son in all the ways that he could. At the same time his mind, where the blood was not thumping at all, realised: Here is the past! It's not the humiliating, defeating past I've spent the last years trying to awake from, with intermittent success and a lot of failure. Violet is the true-hearted past that I lived with Philip and with her and with other friends, a past that was a bit complicated on occasion but was for the most part vivid and cheerful, certainly not utterly to be despised.

In order to bring them both back onto ground that might with more immediate usefulness be walked on, Hugh said: 'Robert is bright, of course he is . . . But do we yet know how bright? Is he any good at exams? Does he have ideas about what he might like to do in due course?'

'Oh – since you ask – as a matter of fact, he does seem to find exams quite straightforward. Comes top all the time, or nearly top nearly all the time. We've had, I've had, other worries about . . . Well, for instance, it would be nice if he had more friends. He's become very solitary, which he wasn't as a little boy. As for what he might want to get up to in years to come . . . He wants to go to his father's and your old college – almost inevitably, I suppose.' To Hugh's relief, she sat down across the room from him, gave him a smile and sipped the brandy he had poured her. 'After which, and because of course he knows he's never going to be able to conduct an existence that much resembles how Philip lived ... It's only fair that you should be warned, he's longing to pluck up the courage to ask you about the sort of thing that you do. To which I should add that not long ago when I asked him if he thought he had any special talents or longings, he left the whole question of longings most sensibly unanswered, but muttered something about how if he had any talent for anything it was merely for day-dreaming. No, don't say it!' Violet was on her feet again, yanking another cigarette from her case. 'You were about to drawl something about how, if he's good at working with his mind and yet all he can really do is day-dream, he's not much better than you are yourself and he'll do brilliantly in government service, in one branch of that or in another – that's right, isn't it? And it's true, he does remind me of you occasionally. By the way, he's fallen heels over head for that pretty Gloria. And apparently Francesco has promised to teach them both to row, day after day they're going to vanish away together in an old skiff, so – well, it doesn't sound the sort of dallying that's absolutely *bound* to have severely anaphrodisiac effects, does it? What sort of girl has she turned into? I haven't seen her since she was a child.'

'She's a delightful girl – unsurprisingly enough, seeing who her mother and father are.'

'Delightful, you say? Ah ...' Plainly having already lost her brief interest in Gloria Venier, Violet at the windows swung around on one heel and came striding back toward

him. 'God almighty, how I've missed you! But the real devil
of it is, the real devil of Philip's being dead is . . . No, it's all
a muddle of different bedevilments. And these veering moods
of mine! Reasonably in control, then idiotically distraught
from one minute to the next, back in perfectly presentable
control, then crazy again.'

She flicked a lighter before her face, she drew a deep breath
of smoke. 'So ridiculous, these swings and roundabouts! All
this jumping onto the merry-go-round and jumping off it,
generally on account of who's got wealth of some sort or
who's been shot, on account of whether you were born first
or whether you were born a boy or a girl, whether you're
someone that other people *have* to haul into their beds or
you're not, whether you've dolled up your sensuality and your
self-centredness with respectable romantic twitter or you
haven't. Honestly, poor Maud! – have you thought of her at
all? Just imagine her returning to Brack after all these years
now that her son has inherited, going back to the house she
ran away from in despair because of Philip's infidelities, to
the house that she can only set foot in again now that the
man she married because she was in love with him has been
killed. You quite liked her, didn't you? Who knows? – perhaps
she and I will meet one day. We never have. The first wife,
the second wife. It's one of those embarrassing, imbecilic
relationships that no two people should ever have, wouldn't
you say? But maybe she'll be coming through the churchyard
at Brack one winter afternoon, going to help arrange the
flowers for one of her grandchildren's christenings or something like that, and she'll notice a madwoman kneeling in

the muddy grass by a small grave. That'll be me. I shan't ever go back to Brack in my life, except perhaps for that reason. That was one of the things, Hugh, that I wasn't very good at coping with in those first days after that War Office telegram came, and I'm still not very good at coping with it. Never to be able to go again to kneel by Clementine's grave. Not to be able to go back to where Philip and I stood that – that – oh God! – that day beside that little pit the sexton had dug. Oh, I'll tell you things you don't know, that you haven't imagined! Or perhaps I won't. Listen – one thing that you probably know the answer to,' she said quite calmly, sitting down again in the shadows on the other side of the room. 'What was the real reason why Philip was hopeless at being married to Maud, right from the start as far as I was ever able to make out? Whereas not a great many years later he was – well – he and I had our wobbles, but nine tenths of the time we were terrific. Was it what I imagine?'

'That in his early twenties he wouldn't have been capable of making any girl a half-way decent husband, but by the time he met you he was ready to fall in love for good? Well, that's what I've always thought.'

She nodded, she tapped her teeth with the amber mouth-piece of her cigarette-holder. 'Chance again! Good luck, bad luck!'

With a smile in his voice, he asked: 'Violet, that holder you're fidgeting with . . . Is it the one I remember from years back, the one that you lost one day out hunting but then somebody found, the one that was famous for having disasters happen to it?'

145

'Just shows that you shouldn't ride to harriers with a little silver stick between your lips, doesn't it? We'd checked by Scarrow Wood and of course I'd lit a cigarette and other people had taken out their flasks. Then suddenly the hounds were off again in full cry. What a gallop! Well worth any number of trinkets. We didn't draw breath for what seemed like a parish and a half. Oh yes, it's the same old one. This thing has been galloped over by horses, it's been dropped on ski slopes and on grouse moors, it's had misadventures at dances and been discovered the next day in compromising circumstances. Once it spent a month in *Calypso*'s bilges. Another time, after a house party at Brack, it was taken back to London by mistake by such a nice woman – she was having an affair with one of Philip's House of Commons friends, they'd spent the weekend hatching some stratagem or other. No, but what I wanted to say was . . .

'After Philip was killed, for a while he was so close to me still! I went on talking to him about everything in the way that I always had – you can imagine, I know you can. But all the while what was dreadful was that I knew in those first days after his death that we'd never be even that close again. I went on with – oh – our jokes and the sort of stories we'd both liked. I went on telling him everything that happened, telling him how brave Robbie was being. I asked him what he wanted me to do. All these years to get through, probably. I went on with my silly murmurings to him. But I knew that even this wasn't going to continue for long. It was simply a question of time passing, of life coming between us. We'd be driven farther and farther apart, our voices would echo

in my head more and more faintly. The dead go on dying
away and dying away – that's one thing I've learned. By the
time I'm an old woman, think how nebulous he'll be! And
now, whatever becomes of me . . . Oh, Hugh, you'll keep a
kind of vague eye on me, won't you? I . . . I sort of promised him I'd turn to you. No, don't say anything. I know you
will.

'I've been brave too,' she went on hurriedly, 'so you don't
need to be ashamed of me. All manner of plans, Robbie and
I have been making! Plans to go to places that Philip and I
never quite got to and to other places that we never got back
to. Stony little Susa up in the Alps, where the Emperor
Augustus built a triumphal arch when he made a treaty with
the old kings of the mountains . . . Have you ever been there?
The peaks around the town flush rose-coloured when the sun
is going down. At least, that was what was happening the
evening Philip and I arrived. There's a grey river that comes
rollicking down. You'd like it. Mass was being said in the
cathedral. We went in, carrying Robbie. About one, he must
have been, your godson. I remember a ruined castle too, and
a baroque church in some vineyards, and chestnut trees –
horse-chestnuts not sweet chestnuts, I think. Philip and I had
always said we'd get back to Susa sooner or later, so now
. . . Well, Robbie and I will go without him.'

Violet was quiet. Then she gave a light sigh. 'It's late. Will
you show me downstairs to your boat?'

Hugh nodded. But for a minute he didn't stir, his heart
steady and his mind more still, more translucent than it had
felt for a long time.

'It occurs to me, Violet, that faced with Philip's death, and with the deaths of all the men who were loved . . . Faced with how much of who we used to be before the war has been obliterated . . . Well, at all events, here's one thing that I seem to think. We'll sit here, and we'll sit on other nights in other places, in England, in France, it doesn't matter where. I don't mean you and I particularly, though we too. All of us who feel lost and feel haunted. A bunch of rememberers, that's who we'll end up having been. It'll be winter and we'll stand up from our hearths to look out at the constellations, or we'll mutter that these cloudy nights you can't see the moon let alone a few stars to lift your heart. Or it'll be a summer night and someone will open a window and someone else will complain about the mosquitoes. We'll take up our meandering talk again, just telling it as it comes. And it won't be altogether futile, I think I've realised, and it won't all be irredeemably sad, and I'll tell you why. It's because what endures will all be there in our stories and will be given different, changing life in them, given renewed life – everything, the griefs, the happinesses, the disillusionments, the need for joy.'

'Oh yes, yes!' she breathed, her eyes bright.

He smiled ruefully, to dispel his already wisping inspiration.

Sent on her way from the Ca' Zante jetty in the gondola, Violet forgot Hugh at once, remembering Philip, and then remembering that there'd been music at night on this Grand Canal for more than a thousand years. She thought how there'd been dances and fallings in love behind these facades and on this water, there'd been tremulous hopes. Oh, they could dig up the earth of twenty countries for soldiers' grave-yards, do it generation after generation. But weren't the old dances still stepping and twirling themselves away in some heaven somewhere? No, of course not . . . but the idea made her rub her knuckle across her eyes.

Turning back indoors after waving his visitor goodbye, Hugh stood stock-still in the hall for a minute, thinking not of Violet or of Philip but of their son – of that tall, quiet boy, fatherless now and homeless, clever apparently, a bit of a dreamer. So he thought Gloria was irresistible, did he? Sensible lad, quite right. And he thought that after Trinity, conceivably the Foreign Office . . . Well, he was going to need a career of some sort, that was for sure. And his godfathers were going to have to pull their weight, going to have to try to be rather more effective presences in his life from now on – which essentially meant he himself, Giacomo Venier not being in formidable shape.

So far, he hadn't been much of a godfather, now that he thought about it. He'd taken Robert for a day's cricket at the Oval and at Lord's a few times. He'd taken him for lunch at his club one day last summer. That sort of thing. But if they were to become friends in time to come . . .

Idolatry, that's what it is, he thought, suddenly knowing what it was he'd say to Robert Mancroft in maybe ten years, if Violet was right that the boy and he had a few strengths and weaknesses in common, if Robert were to happen to join the Foreign Office, if ever there were to come into being between the two of them an echoing to and fro of sympa-thies and ideas. The fascination of a difficult profession,

the love of your country and the readiness to serve, the love
of women, the delight you take in the arts, the delight that
perhaps you take in old houses or in landscapes or in the
sea . . . It all just means, he thought, that you've got more
self-understanding to wake up to bitterly afterward, to wake
up to when it's too late for that particular knowledge to be
of any help – because the kaleidoscope never interrupts its
marvels for your sake, the apparitions go on evolving, you
need new perceptions all the time not your old ones. Graven
images! he thought. Idolatry, that's all it is! The more you've
cast your heart into, the more territory of self-recognition
and self-contempt there is for you to map afterward, that's
all there is to it. Poor boy!

XVIII

Elena, traipsed after and sporadically assisted by Donatella, had swept and dusted the upper *sala*, which the family had not used for decades, so that Giacomo Venier, now that his heart was so much weaker, should have his own domain, at the core of his house and yet secluded from the life of his family in the *sala* below. All through May, the defective engine in his chest had seemed to pump his blood more and more feebly. He sat by the windows over the Grand Canal, propped up on silk cushions in a rattan chair with a foot-rest, which was how he said he felt most comfortable, though in fact he liked that particular chair because thirty-odd years before it had been shipped back from Eritrea, in those days a new colony, by his brother Daniele who had been soldiering there. Valentina had noticed that now that death had taken another unmistakable stride toward him, her husband liked to have things by him that were redolent of those he had loved long ago. The little table that he'd asked to have placed beside his chair had been his mother's, and on it he had her travelling clock and the oil lamp she'd had at her bedside all through her widowhood. When he'd wanted to read some Verga, he'd asked to be brought his father's edition.

Giacomo had not had another heart-attack, though he couldn't help remembering the one he'd had a couple of years before; on his bad days, when he was too weak to receive visitors or even to read, he'd sit there hoping that it might be possible to leave life without that being repeated. There was also the danger that he might have a stroke (without mentioning this to each other, Dr Zanon and his patient had both come to the conclusion that he'd already had a slight one), and it was difficult not to keep imagining that too.

Giacomo had been sluggish and contemplative for years, but these were times when his whole consciousness seemed to him to have become passive: it was like the unclean lagoon where the tides feebly flowed and feebly ebbed but nothing else occurred. Or his consciousness would present itself to him in the image of the impoverished, decaying city at the heart of which he sat, helpless and painful, at his windows above the water traffic. All he'd be aware of was his own weakened thinking, and his Venice where, since the Republic fell, generations had been born and had died, but all attempts at freedom and at regeneration had failed; his Venice where people came to have a look at the imposing carcass of a state and went away again; his Venice that had gone terribly inert and quiet, where nothing ever happened except damage.

These were hours and days when so little vital force was pumped up from Giacomo's heart to his head that he took to wearing an old velvet fez, even in warm weather, to stop his skull feeling frighteningly cold. It was a crimson fez with a black tassel, which Valentina had unearthed for him from a cupboard in a bedroom where nobody had slept since she could remember. At these times, when his desanguinated thoughts could not achieve anything or fend anything off, he liked to have his wife or one of his children sit with him.

To everybody's relief, Francesco had reacted to the crisis with commendable maturity. He was in the law faculty at nine o'clock every morning, and he had already announced that this summer, instead of regattas and instead of the Lido and tennis and swimming, he was going to work. He'd spoken to his father's partner at the practice near Rialto, who had promised to keep him busy with jobs in the office and to give him every chance of beginning to get the hang of the profession.

So usually it was Valentina who sat in the armchair drawn up to face Giacomo's rattan chair. And as soon as Gloria came home from school, she'd hurry up to the second floor. The girl had never cared for a sick man before, but she took to it simply and naturally. She brought him the small meals that were all he wanted: a bowl of game or fish soup, bread wrapped in a napkin, a glass of wine. She dabbed the eau-de-Cologne that he liked on the silk handkerchiefs he wore in the breast pockets of his old-fashioned suits. When he wanted to shuffle as far as the bathroom, or when it was time for him to go to bed, she helped him to his feet and they set off together, he with his stick in one hand and his other hand on her shoulder.

When he felt up to it, Gloria and her father talked as much

as they always had. When he was too weak, she'd see this as soon as her quick steps brought her down the length of the upper *sala* toward where he sat in silhouette against the daylight. If his head was laid back against the cushions, if the volume of Turgenev or of Verga or whoever he'd been reading had been put down on the table, she'd know they were going to be quiet. 'Papa,' she'd say simply, and he'd reply, 'Gloria' – their greeting never changed. Long before midsummer, she'd got used to spending half her free time sitting opposite his baggy old frame slumped in its rattan chair. It felt right to her, to keep watch over his bony fore-head, his slack jowls, his drowsing eyes. She could partake of the life of the Grand Canal just as well from that row of contiguous windows as she could from her sole bedroom window on the floor above. Sometimes she'd pick up one of the books on his table and read it. Sometimes she'd stand up, kick her stiff legs and stretch her arms, lean against one of the columns and muse.

All through his decline, Giacomo Venier went on being visited by old friends from the Italian mainland and from France, from Austria and from England, who would not have dreamed of being in Venice without looking up Valentina and him. As for local people, he was called upon by families from the whole gamut of that stagnant society. Tradesmen and professors and boatmen, the mayor and his wife, the countess who ran the Venetian branch of the Red Cross, the woman in his office who'd typed his letters, magistrates and booksellers, the priest from the Greek church – then rich, swanky people in industry and poor, swanky people in the theatre ... They all wanted to know how he was, they all wanted to know how Valentina was bearing up and whether they might offer help of some kind.

Often old acquaintances would bump into each other at the Veniers' water-gate or in the alley behind the house. At once starting to catch up on their news, they'd go upstairs together to the lower *sala* where, if it was one of Giacomo's bad days, the family would sit them down. But if he was feeling better, in the early evenings the master of the house would hold his modest court on the second storey. Friends would be urged to draw up a chair, or in fine weather to prop themselves on the balustrade over the water. They'd be offered a glass of vermouth from the lacquer tray on the sideboard.

It was scarcely possible for his friends to convince themselves that Giacomo Venier was ever going to make a recovery. On the other hand, there were summer evenings when it was irresistible to conclude that the old fellow was wearing his crimson fez not because he was cold but because he'd rather taken a fancy to that Levantine headgear. There'd be a cheerful atmosphere as his friends silently reminded themselves that after all he *hadn't* had a further heart-attack, he was merely a lot weaker, and that Dr Zanon had often proved an expert at prolonging the most precarious existences. You never knew, this last, rattan-chair season of Venier's life might go on for a year or two, perhaps even longer.

On one of his better evenings, the dying man might hitch himself more upright, tweak down his cuffs, reach for his spectacles, and read aloud Hugh Thurne's latest letter from Paris or London. (Thurne had not been back in Venice since

Easter, but Valentina and he were in communication. And he made a point of writing to Giacomo most weeks with his latest thoughts about this brand new League of Nations, which sounded wonderful on paper, or his thoughts about the web of peace settlements that was supposed to be going to hold the Old World in uneasy amity, the last dispiriting threads of which were still being spun by cob spiders such as himself.) And to the end of his life, Giacomo Venier always wanted to know his city's news. He'd join happily in local talk about quays that hadn't been repaired since God knew when and were losing chunks of masonry, about a promising dancer rumoured to be about to join the *corps de ballet*, about a fishing fleet caught in a storm.

This evening he was feeling stronger than he had of recent days. Gloria was off somewhere. Nobody had arrived, but he was expecting Valentina, who all afternoon had been at Ca' Zante, where for nearly a month Violet Mancroft had been installed on the top floor. (Robert, dispatched back across the continent after Easter by train to Dover, London and Eton, would return to his mother in July.)

XIX

Giacomo Venier's money difficulties; what would happen to Valentina and Francesco and Gloria in years to come; whether it might be necessary to let or even to sell part of his house – all these perplexities, which had dogged him so mercilessly, now scarcely dogged him at all, because he was finished, he was out of it. Other people would have to cope, and therefore they would cope – or at least they'd have a chance to try, which he wouldn't.

He was tiredly aware that his wife had had consultations with the accountant, with various old friends of the family, with Francesco and even with Gloria. But he himself was not consulted any more; he was reassured, which was different. He was aware that the next time Hugh Thurne was in Rome, Francesco was going to meet him there, because although a solid training in jurisprudence never did a young man any harm, it didn't mean he necessarily had to be a provincial lawyer for the rest of his days; there'd be absolutely no harm in him being introduced to men in politics and men in government service, and no harm either in him meeting one or two of the society hostesses who counted. Giacomo had been told this in order that it should encourage him, and he had been encouraged. But this evening this being already excluded and this being given only reassuring news afforded him a dour satisfaction and even amusement. Yes, this must be one of the ways in which life prepared you for death. And it *was* merciful; you *did* begin to care less. When all there was left for you was to sit here, far too conscious of the heart in your chest and of the brain in your head, listening to the Grand Canal belfries chime the hours as they had all your life, waiting for something to go hideously wrong either behind your ribs or behind your eyes – oh, it was merciful.

All the ideas too, the disputations about the past, the anxieties about the country in the future – what a relief to have it matter less! Even if the reason for its diminished importance, for its recession from you, was that soon you yourself were going to stop mattering less each day and start not mattering at all. Just imagine how ridiculous, to have sat with your friends – in the twentieth century, for heaven's sake! – and to have mulled over how back in the 1790s Venice and indeed the other Italian states might quite feasibly have been saved, if a formidable army had been maintained at, say, Verona and impressive garrisons in the other mainland cities, if a fighting alliance against the invading French had been formed with the Emperor of Austria and with the Kings of Naples and Sardinia. Honestly, when that sort of talk started up among their elders, Francesco and his generation were quite right to smile behind their hands and waggle their eyebrows.

As recently as Easter, he had still been fretting about how, less than a year after the triumph of Italian arms against Austria at the battle of Vittorio Veneto, already on the mainland both the Nationalists and the Socialists were getting more bloodthirsty and more half baked every time you opened your morning newspaper, the rule of law appeared to be well on its way to breaking down, the national political putrescence was fairly plain to see. Well, now Francesco and Gloria were going to have to fret about that, not him!

Daniele Venier had been killed at Adowa in '96, when the Italian army had been advancing into Abyssinia and had been massacred. His body had never been identified, or indeed, probably, ever been buried. Now, instead of raging against that misguided invasion as he had used to, his brother was smiling as he recollected how even half a century ago this upper *sala* had not been in use – so it had been perfect for a couple of scamps who wanted to play leapfrog undisturbed, and wanted to build the furniture into fences for their imaginary thoroughbreds, and build a booby-trap for the English governess when she should come to rout them out.

Valentina still had not returned. Giacomo went on musing in his detached, reminiscent way about the room he was in, from which two Marieschi oil paintings that Daniele would have remembered had vanished, leaving discoloured oblongs on the walls – he'd sold them himself, seven or eight years ago, to pay for he couldn't now remember what. So much had been sold from this city! – by him, by his father, by his grandfather, by thousands not much better or worse than them. Marble well-heads, libraries of Renaissance books,

altars, columns, scientific instruments and musical instruments beyond counting, cabinets and tapestries and weaponry
beyond counting, work in silver and gold and glass, whole
painted ceilings, even staircases, anything that could be transmuted into cash. Barges freighted with urns and busts, he'd
seen, passing in front of this house on their way to the railway
station.

They'd sold to pay their daughters' dowries, they'd sold
so that their ineffectual sons could keep up a pointless yet
pleasant style of life – or was that not fair? When a society
had failed to defend its economic self-sufficiency and its
political independence it was done for, Venice had become a
backwater of Italy quite naturally and quickly. That wasn't
the problem. The problem was that Italy was a backwater of
Europe. And the worst of it these last hundred and twenty
years wasn't the dozens of churches and palaces pulled down,
the canals filled in to make streets, the wide thoroughfares
lined with dead-alive nineteenth-century buildings driven
though the mediaeval quarters, the marble fireplaces that
cropped up in sale rooms in Paris and London, though all
that was wretched enough. What was it Hugh had said once,
in that firm, laconic way of his? Something about how . . .
Oh look, there was Gloria in that little boat of hers with her
cousin Stefano. Something about how, after the traditions of
independence and pride were gone, after the tumbling down
of a house of cards on the scale of the Venetian Republic's
tumbling down, other societies would take up the running
and good luck to them. But where you were, the intellectual
zest would be gone, the tradition of supreme achievement

would be gone and that was sad. Well, well, so those two were going boating together! The trouble was, she'd taken a terrific shine to Robbie Mancroft. Well, that girl's heart was probably going to turn a fair number of somersaults in the coming years. In preparation for which, so that her throat should be suitably adorned while she was precipitating young men toward despair, he had looked out a necklace of garnets that had been her grandmother's for her birthday next week.

When at Easter his daughter's and his godson's shy beguilement had become manifest, to their mothers' relief Giacomo had been amused and charmed. In his rumbling voice he'd made remarks about how the lad must be nearly the age of Shakespeare's Romeo, while Gloria was older than – could she possibly be? yes, older – than Juliet. But he was fond of Gloria and Francesco's second cousin Stefano Moretta, who was going to inherit the small estate at La Badia and who, he suspected, would let himself realise how much he liked Gloria if she ever gave him a hint of encouragement.

Stefano had gone out to the Horn of Africa straight after school to work in some humble capacity in the colonial administration – clerking, or some such, Giacomo had an idea. But then after three years on the Somali coast, with his parents ill and La Badia no longer on the battle-front, he'd come home. With an equal readiness to work hard at what came to hand, he'd started to try to make something of those war-damaged properties and unprofitable acres. So Giacomo in his old-fashioned manner approved of the young man's spirit. He'd even imagined that the sensible thing – but, of course, these days you couldn't organise other people's lives for them, you just couldn't – would be for Gloria and him to be married one day.

The rattan chair faced east; Giacomo commanded the long reach of the Grand Canal from San Stae opposite his windows down toward Rialto. For minutes, he watched the *sandolo* (which had been repainted blue and grey with a red water-line, and had become his daughter's exclusive property and her command) as it set off toward the market, the young man sitting on the thwart and facing aft so they could talk, Gloria in the stern standing at her oar.

Valentina and he had got used to being rowed by their son in the family gondola, Giacomo thought, smiling at the scene below him – but just imagine being rowed by a female member of the family! None of Gloria's girlfriends would dream of taking up oarsmanship, as she'd done this year with tremen-dous enthusiasm and panache; it just wasn't a thing young ladies did. Perhaps she *was* going to be rather a handful. Still, how seductive and how tantalising for Stefano to have his pretty cousin take him for a wander through the canals on a kingfisher-coloured evening.

Giacomo Venier sighed, realising that what he'd thought earlier was only half true. He wasn't going to die so numbed, indifferent, peaceful as all that. When it came to two things, when it came to his city and his daughter, he minded all right.

Suddenly sensing that on the floors beneath him Valentina had returned, he frowned, reminded of the houses on the Grand Canal that were no longer lived in by the families who'd owned them when he was a boy. There were his friends at Ca' Zante and there were a handful of other newcomers too, whom he knew but less well: French, American, English, down toward San Marco for the most part, not up here in Cannaregio. Edmond de Polignac's widow, what was her name? – even in a scandalous city, she'd made people twitter and chuckle. And that delightful Prince von Hohenlohe, with whom he'd got on so well before the war – it would be nice if now that they were all at peace again he came back. Oh, of course it was fine, the selling of houses, the dividing of houses into flats, the new people. But things were changing. And it was also not fine. Hotels too, they were a blight.

The Grand Canal wasn't the residential highway, one of the hearts of Venetian life, that it had been even at the end of the last century. There weren't all the children's parties there'd been, or that was his impression. There wasn't so much neighbourly coming and going all day and half the night between the water-gates. There weren't the weddings and the christenings, the . . . Well, his own funeral was going to be the kind of Grand Canal occasion he approved of; this would be a contribution he could make to shoring things up futilely for a little.

Of course Gloria could have a floor of this house. Francesco and whomever he married couldn't possibly need the whole place. If Gloria married a local fellow like her cousin, if she married someone like Robert and gadded off across the world – it made no difference.

But after that, if her brother and she both had children, what was going to happen? You couldn't divide the place up indefinitely. Sooner or later, somebody who'd been born on this Grand Canal was going to have to achieve something,

or else ... and under the present political conditions ...!
But perhaps these plans for a big modern port would be
successful. It was even conceivable that the ship-building
industry might be revived at long last – or wasn't it, not after
all these years? Damned old Hugh was right: barges loaded
with statues and urns passing below your windows on their
way elsewhere, that was what you got if you had let yourselves be defeated, ever since Babylon. And by way of clout
in this world, a brace of comic local politicians posted down
to Rome to be corrupted and fooled.

XX

Giacomo Venier sat with a bitter, amused light in his eyes, watching his daughter and her skiff get smaller and smaller in the distance, every fibre in his being wishing her well for all the years she'd live without him. Only last Easter, that day when they'd all been on the water together, he'd been immobilised by how precarious they all were, how tenuously held together this intersection of their lives was. It had been one of the spirit's strange intermittences; for a minute he'd been suffused by intimations that must have been forming where they were invisible to him, because suddenly the obscurity had gone and there they'd been. Well, predictably enough he was the one who'd turned out to be a lot more precarious than the rest; his was the vision of things that was going to be dispelled first. He wouldn't for much longer be taking an interest in how his intimations formed themselves.

Gloria had disappeared. With a wry smile on his lips, he turned his gaze back into the room, to things he'd known all his life, things that hadn't been sold – a marquetry bureau,

a sofa covered in tatty brocade, a wall where some etchings
by Guido Reni had always hung and still hung. It was silly
to feel sorry for inanimate things that you were about to
abandon, but he did. The bronze Venus that stood in the
middle of the drum table, an ivory statuette of an Indian
goddess that had been a favourite of his. Or was it that right
now the very materials these helpless things were made of
seemed dreadfully sad for some reason? Wood, cloth, the
glass and wire of the chandelier, things made of china and
made of leather. More wood, more cloth . . . all this worked
matter, waiting for whatever was going to be done with it.
Ugh! – it was all wrong for his mood this evening. These
wretchedly material things, waiting to be cherished and given
new meaning by people not yet born, or waiting to be repaired,
or waiting (these pockmarked, ribbony curtains that had
been his grandmother's) to be judged beyond repair and
thrown out. Frowning with perplexity, he shuddered. And
how stupid to be distressed by things simply being what they
were, by inlaid walnut being inlaid walnut, scuffed brocade
being scuffed brocade.

Valentina came in. Approaching him down the long room,
she reassured herself at a glance that he was still feeling as
relatively strong as he had been after lunch when she had left
the house. 'Darling,' she said, stooping to kiss him on his
temple just below the rim of his fez.

She had made her way home across the city on foot,
enjoying the streets and the people shopping and the views
from the bridges as she had done all her life. But at the same
time she'd been thinking of Violet, with whom she'd spent

the afternoon, who'd been widowed in her late thirties; and she'd carried along in her head her own probable fate, the almost certainty that, if she didn't lose Giacomo this summer when she wasn't yet fifty, well, it was too much to hope that she'd have him when she was old.

She'd walked thinking of her twenty-five years of wanderings along these quays with him, in an ache of misery that they would never do this again. She'd reminded herself that Philip and Giacomo had both been lucky, when she thought of the hundreds of thousands of young soldiers who'd been killed when they were still more boys than men. Yes, yes, she knew, she knew . . . But if only Giacomo and she could have had another twenty years, however ill and hard-up they'd been, if only they could have grown old side by side, what thanks she would have given!

Valentina sat down opposite him in Gloria's and her invariable place, looking into the roseate shimmer left in the sky by the sun which, behind the houses and beyond the western lagoon, was sinking toward the land. Since Giacomo had chosen to have his rattan chair positioned toward the east, his head at this hour of the evening was already beginning to be in shadow. (And if he wished to read, his brass lamp had to be lit.) But his companion, his wife or his daughter, always had the faint flush of the evening on her face.

'Violet has really made it extremely attractive, that top floor,' Valentina began, seeing from his alert eyes that he wasn't feeling too ghastly and would like to hear how her afternoon had been. 'She's got a couple of lemon trees in tubs on the loggia, there are a lot of improvements since I last went to see her. Of course, there's no kitchen or dining-room up there, which is a bore. Apparently what happens is that, for lunch the housekeeper dishes up something for her in the dining-room, and in the evening Violet goes to the kitchen and muddles around and looks after herself. She said that tonight she was going to poach herself a couple of eggs and either eat them at the kitchen table or plod all the way up to the loggia with them – the kitchen in that house is on the ground floor, you probably remember. But that all sounds all right, wouldn't you say? And – well, you know how ropy her Italian is. But she's going to lessons five days a week and she seems to be enjoying that. So one way and another . . . I know she's very solitary. But that's inevitable. And in many ways it's right for her this year, it's a kindness. And she *is* beginning to see a few people as well as you and me, and this will increase, slowly. So – all in all, I think it promises well.'

'When Hugh comes back, presumably they'll lunch and dine together, when neither of them has been invited else-where.'

'Oh, my love . . . The longer he stays away the better!' Valentina's fine black eyes, which were all the beauty she had left, sparkled with her delight in her idea. Her voice kindled. 'If I had my way, or possibly I mean if I had more courage, I'd tell him to leave her be for a couple of years at least, and then just to pitch up for a week, merely to remind her that he still exists, before disappearing again.'

She leaned her head back and rested it; for a few moments she hesitated. But then she burst out in a soft, thrilling voice that the man listening to her hadn't heard for a long time.

'Giacomo, my darling, sometimes I'm tortured by hope! – for you and me, that we should be spared for as long as possible, and for others too. For Francesco and Gloria, naturally – but also for all manner of friends of ours, for Violet, for Hugh. I *refuse* to be afraid and gloomy and nothing else. Who knows? – perhaps the worst is past for a lot of people. Perhaps the twenties of this century are going to be a glorious time, are going to be terrific – it's possible, isn't it? – why shouldn't they be? And even here in this rotting Venice of ours too, here where a lot of Francesco and Gloria's future is going to be played out, or so I imagine. I dare say I'm losing my wits, but at times I think that, now that the war is over, the two of them stand a chance of having a lot of fun.'

Valentina Venier was utterly oblivious of how, by an inexorable inverse process, as her husband had become rapidly more debilitated, she had become less anxious and more resolute; at the eleventh hour of their marriage the balance of psychological strength had tipped decisively. But she was acutely aware of her determination this summer that, whatever happened after Giacomo's death, whether then she went most vilely to pieces or she didn't, while he was still alive she wasn't going to let him down. From her he was going to get the sort of talk they'd always had; he was going to get good sense and bravery as well as tenderness. And this, coupled with her visceral relief that this evening his eyes were glowing, that he seemed to be more his old self than he had lately, made her lean forward in her chair and smile and give his knee a brief, affectionate rub.

'Do you know, darling, as I was coming away from Ca' Zante I met Marcella Zancana, so we walked together as far as a café. By the way, she appears to know for sure that Stefano is going to wait for two years or thereabouts and then ask Gloria if she could bear to marry him. So we're warned, if we needed to be. But that's not the immediate thing. Listen . . . just because no one's come to see us this evening doesn't mean we can't have a glass of something, you and I. Good idea?'

'Good idea. Thank you.'

'Well, it turns out that Marcella knows this singer that Hugh's been tangled up with, and apparently she truly is rather fantastic to look at, which I imagine explains events. But the real news is . . . Oh Lord! Well, just for a change, it doesn't seem to be Hugh who's behaving shabbily, or not only him.'

Valentina had lived with such contented and immaculate constancy herself that, despite not being a prude and despite having passed her adult life in friendly contact with a fair number of men and women who might have considerable virtues but not that of immaculacy, she still on occasion wavered when she had actually to speak of others' carryings on, so now she took the opportunity of standing up and going to the sideboard to pour two glasses of vermouth. Watching her, Giacomo thought: Oh good, she's in strong heart, she probably *will* be all right when I'm dead.

'It seems that . . . You remember the conductor Amedeo Della Rovere who's here? He's living at the Excelsior for the season, and naturally half the young women who ever have

occasion to go waltzing in and out of the Fenice have been
. . . oh, the predictable chattering has been going on and the
predictable quivering. Well, according to Marcella, the young
lady that Hugh likes has been one of those not rebuffed.
Which in many respects is a good thing. Apparently Della
Rovere and she have been dallying merrily on the Lido, at
least occasionally.'

Valentina was frowning so puzzledly and yet so cheerfully
as she handed him his glass and sat down again that Giacomo,
who had often asked himself whether she knew that for years
she'd been half in love with Hugh Thurne, wondered instead
whether now she'd stumbled on a new, less hurtful manner
of loving him, and whether in time she would realise this.

'Because Hugh can't persist like this indefinitely, can he?
I can't help being afraid that his endless liaisons will end up
by making him a little laughable – or do I sound horribly
old-fashioned? The trouble, according to Marcella, is that
he's been exceedingly fascinated by her. But now, when he
finds out that she isn't his romantic darling . . . Because of
course, along with all the other abominable complications,
as you'll readily imagine it will be intolerable for Violet if
whenever he's in Venice he uses Ca' Zante to entertain his
latest mistresses. He really will have to put all that behind
him.'

'Valentina my love, perhaps in your enthusiasm for your
new idea you shouldn't forget that, reprehensibly perhaps but
these are the facts, men have not invariably ceased to be
obsessed by beautiful women just because they couldn't have
them to themselves. Women, indeed, are not immensely more

rational in these matters. Further, in your enthusiasm for Violet and for Hugh you seem to have forgotten that he already has a wife.'

'Oh, that doesn't matter. If one fine day Hugh and Violet are married or if they never are – it won't make a scrap of difference. I say, have you noticed how marvellously immoral I'm getting to be? A disgusting old match-maker who doesn't even insist primly on the social decencies, that's me. No, what counts is . . . Well, one thing: the way she is when she's talking about him, though of course she hasn't a clue how from her every gesture and her every word it transpires how essential for her he is. And this will take a long time even to reach a beginning. Violet isn't one of those war widows aged twenty-two who, after six months of crying their eyes out, a couple of years later marry their first husband's best friend who was in the same regiment with him or in the same ship. She loved Philip with all her heart and she was married to him for nearly twenty years. She'll never recover conclusively from that, nor should she, and it'll take a while for her to see beyond it.'

Valentina was smiling ruefully at him with her lips, to show that she too understood that all this might easily turn out to be nonsense. But Giacomo was watching the very different confident, amused glimmer in her eyes, which rejoiced his heart when he thought of how she would be afterward, in years to come.

'What will count will be whether Hugh can stop making a fool of himself with lover after lover young enough to be his daughter; whether Violet can live in quiet and freedom at Ca' Zante and then, when he's there for a few days or a few weeks, she can get to know him all over again, discover him in a new, changed way. What will count will be whether he can let her know that, somewhere on the haziest of horizons, he's there, and whether she can let him understand the same thing. *If you want my life, come and take it* – do you remember that line? It's in *The Seagull,* isn't it? – it's somewhere in Chekhov. I have a notion you once said it was a line that had stayed with you. That Violet and Hugh should be there for one another in the future, perhaps very discreetly and intermittently, perhaps not, that's up to them. Because those two could love each other very truly, given time, there's no question of that. Oh I don't know, my old sweetheart, am I making any sense at all?'

'A little, possibly. I'm not sure. Certainly if Violet goes to roost at Ca' Zante for some years, or even if she roosts there until she dies of old age, in the short term this will be pleasant and propitious for Robert and Gloria. Had you thought of that? I expect you had. And – if none of this works out? For instance, if Hugh has been behaving all these years in ways that are natural to him and if he doesn't change? If Violet finds existence at Ca' Zante a little distasteful and by, oh, shall we say by next winter, has pushed off?'

'Then I think it could all become sad rather quickly. Hugh would be left with his sham marriage, with a lot of hypocrisy, with his so-called love affairs. Violet . . . Oh, for a couple of years she might come and go between Paris and the coast of Normandy. Then for another season of her life she might try London again, or it'd be Tuscany. Worse, almost at once it wouldn't any longer be her giving Robert amusing holidays, it'd be him having to squire her around. Eventually she'd have a few flings, even a – oh, what do I mean? – a marriage not at the level of the spirit she's got.'

XXI

Emanuela Zuccarelli had begun her affair with Amedeo Della Rovere for the sufficient reasons that he was famous and that, of the handful of conductors in the land who'd been given standing ovations in Naples and Rome and Milan, men who might favourably influence a young singer's career, he was still only in early middle age and he was not physically repellent. Or, perhaps, they had seduced one another merely because they both happened to be knocking around on the Lido this season, they both had the habit of seduction, they were feeling a bit listless, they felt they deserved cheering up and could do with some fun.

Emanuela didn't know what was wrong with her this summer, but something was. Before, when Hugh Thurne had been away for week after week, she'd liked how her Venetian life had taken her back, she'd liked the freedom of that. Before, she could have gone to bed a few times with a successful, womanising conductor without at once knowing in her guts how trite and useless this was.

Now she was irritated with Hugh for leaving her alone for so long, and for when he *was* in Venice sometimes truly seeming to be in love with her and making her feel in love with him, at other times being so distracted by his books and his ideas, and being so taken up with this English mother and son whom he appeared to have adopted, that she wanted to shriek. She was irritated with Amedeo because, although he was infinitely more satisfactory than Hugh when it came to inviting her out to lunch at the Hotel des Bains and to dinner at the Excelsior, it had never crossed his mind to be romantic and take her with him when he left Venice at the summer's end; she wasn't going to be singing an important role at La Scala next winter.

She was irritated with herself because this year she *had* let herself feel romantic with Hugh and it hadn't made her happy, or it hadn't yet. She was dissatisfied because the first torrid heat had arrived in late May, so now in July it was sweltering; she felt languid and frivolous and for some reason this was all wrong, though in the past it had been fine enough. Because today Hugh was back at Ca' Zante, he'd sent his gondola for her and she was going to him but she didn't know why. Yes, and because . . . Oh, for Christ's sake, what was the matter with her? If she could only get back her old rhythm of living cheerfully from day to day she'd be all right! – was that it, or wasn't it?

A storm had been in the offing all afternoon. Emanuela emerged onto the sultry, fly-ridden quay reluctantly, because her flat with its pretty furnishings that she had chosen might only be a bolt-hole but at least it was hers and it meant being herself, or at least it would be hers for so long as she could go on paying the rent. She glanced up at the louring cloud-rack and did not unfurl her parasol. She stood there aware of butterflies flittering in her diaphragm, because this good-looking young gondolier Gastone, doing a stint of work for Hugh Thurne, fancied her. Worse, he and she came of the same impoverished Venetian stock. Recognitions had flashed between them the first time their eyes met. He knew she knew that an oarsman that handsome would play the gigolo for visiting heiresses when it was asked of him, as well as having a local fiancée whom he'd marry when this pleasure could not be postponed any longer. She knew he knew that a lot of young women tried to make a career at the Fenice, if they could dance or sing or play the violin, but it was a risky busi-ness at best; most of them never got anywhere worth getting to, so the occasional foreign milord could be helpful.

Gastone reached out his arm so she could steady herself as she came aboard, running his gaze up her body to her face. 'Sorry I'm late,' he said in Venetian rather than Italian. 'Or don't you mind?'

Putting three fingers on his sleeve, Emanuela stepped past him, breathing his faint smell of sweat and sea sunshine. 'It's going to rain before long, Gastone.'

He shrugged.

The black *felze*, the tiny upholstered cabin, which had been removed from the boat during the hot weather, had been reinstalled in view of the impending downpour. Dreading its stuffy enclosedness on such a humid evening, but at the same time welcoming its privacy, Emanuela settled herself on the warm cushions, suddenly defeated by all Hugh's disappearances and reappearances, by the unending changes to what she might expect if she stayed with him, by her own readiness to come running the minute he whistled.

Emanuela left her ornate cabin door open to the oppressive air, so she could look forward past the gondola's prow down the well-loved backwater that in a minute would bring them to Campo dei Mori and the house where Tintoretto had lived. This *felze* was a damned coop. Yes, but when the cloudburst came, which it would any moment now . . . all over the city, craft of all kinds would take shelter under bridges, and aboard others men would grumble and pull on their oilskins and keep going.

Her mind filled with an enticing image of this gondola stationary beneath a bridge as the débâcle of rain broke (as it chanced, no other vessel would be cowering beneath the same protective arch), and the image of Gastone who, with a clatter of his shipped oar and a knowing grin, would come forward and down into the cockpit.

The low cusp of sky Emanuela could see was livid. A clap of thunder startled her. Feeling her nape suddenly icy, she pressed her finger-tips to her throbbing temples, where for days and nights the stupid tensions had clung. Isolated plump drops fell into the mottled water, then nothing again.

Release from all this, she thought, that's what I want. Forget it all, it's none of it any use. Release! Something strong, something sweet. And then forgetfulness. Then a long, long oblivion, and waking up different from this. A new mood, a new time.

A flurry of wind harried ripples across the canal, bumped a floating bottle against the hull. The rain started once more, fitfully, making rings where it fell. Emanuela saw a mad vision; she saw herself dressed in her Tiepolo colours duck out of this cabin in the first of the deluge and go scrambling aft on all fours like an animal. She saw herself clench her arms around Gastone's thighs where he stood at his oar, haul herself up. She felt his arms, she felt his mouth as they stood there held hard, the rain drubbing down on her hair and on his hair, on his cotton shirt and on her silk dress, because he was of her people and she was of his. Or – oh, for God's sake – because . . .

No, no. Yes. Emanuela writhed voluptuously on her cushions. She hoicked aside a fragment of black brocade, scrabbled at the brass catch of her dimity window. This was madness, but it was an ancient, familiar madness, it was good.

The rain's rings on the water were beginning to overlap. Her heart thudding, she heard Gastone's footfalls on the gunwale. Now he was bending down to where her shaking white hand with its rings had made her diminutive opening.

'I . . . You . . .' It was a whisper. She tried again. 'You'll get soaked. Please, please.'

XXII

Emanuela Zuccarelli arrived at Ca' Zante when the sunset after the rainstorm had made the sky iridescent with washed blues and opalescent greeny-greys and rose-flushed greys. Briefly, the air was cool, it smelled of fresh water and drenched foliage.

Waving goodbye gaily to Gastone, who raised his arm in an ironic salutation, she hurried through the hall and out into the garden with its walls overgrown with ivy. The wisteria pergola was dripping profusely all over the wrought-iron table and chairs. The gravel paths and the flower-beds were sodden. The catalpa tree was pitter-pattering water-drops at every flutter of breeze and every sparrow's alighting. No, of course Hugh was never going to have been waiting for her here. He must be indoors – but with his English lady-friend, whom she'd seen from a distance a couple of times coming or going at the palace jetty, or on his own? And why had she come here this evening, and why had she and Gastone. . . ?

Thanks to her ten minutes with Gastone in the *felze*

181

beneath a bridge at no great distance from Campo dei Mori, when she'd stepped ashore at Ca' Zante Emanuela had felt less dissatisfied with life and less dissatisfied with herself than she had for weeks. She'd enjoyed the swing of her legs and the toss of her head as she'd come swanning through the Corinthian hall, because it had instantly been vivid to her that this wasn't half bad, if you could have the odd tumble in a boat and you could also have your love affair, which might go on for years and years, in a palace. What was more . . . Well, these high-heeled red shoes of hers tapping on the marble, the whole elegant swirl of her as she advanced between the pillars – this style of life went with her and she went with it.

But now, less than a hundred seconds after waving to Gastone, she stood petulantly among the drips. Of course if Hugh wanted to introduce her to his English visitor that was fine. But even so, it had been a lot more delightful in the old days when, after the housekeeper went home each afternoon, when she herself had arrived in the evening or late at night, she'd been the only woman in the house. Couldn't Hugh have met her at a restaurant? Couldn't they then have gone back to her flat? How was this all going to work out? Oh, for God's sake, what was the point of this love affair?

'I'm up here, Emanuela!' came Hugh's voice from the loggia three storeys above her. 'Do come up, it's a fabulous evening.'

'Right!' she called, chucking her head back so that through the rose arbour she could just see him leaning on the balustrade up there, on his own it looked like, and then wincing in exasperation when a cascade of drops from the leaves and flowers spattered onto her face. 'Right! Coming!'

Emanuela strode back into the hall. But then, instead of swinging left to the staircase and beginning to go up it, she swung right. She let herself out of the street door. She turned right along the private alley, let herself out of the next gate, kept striding. She crossed the little square beyond Ca' Zante's garden, without glancing behind her and upward to see if in the loggia the man who was expecting her to appear at any moment, sit down, probably accept a glass of champagne, was instead astoundedly regarding her back and the tilt of her hat as she made off into the warren of lanes.

Hugh's and her preferred café on the Zattere was shut, but the tables and chairs outside were still there, a bit disordered, a bit scruffy. She sat down, with no premonition of what she might do next or what she might think, facing the channel across to the Giudecca, on her own, in the glistens of evening, in the lappings of the tide. Then she smiled, thinking something that she hadn't expected to think.

She'd change, utterly. Partly because she'd have to, partly because she'd wish to. The likes of Amedeo Della Rovere and Hugh Thurne weren't going to want her indefinitely, which was rather a relief more than anything else, and perhaps she wasn't going to want them. She'd hang onto her position in the chorus at La Fenice for as long as she could, because even a small pay packet was a whole lot better than nothing, and she'd get a job as a singing teacher too. She knew that just as she'd never be offered leading parts on famous stages, she wouldn't ever be appointed to a prestigious post at the

Conservatory. But there was that small music school at Santa Giustina where she had friends, she'd go along there right now, during the summer holidays, and see if they'd take her on in the autumn to teach singing to a class of children. That would be the sort of work she'd enjoy, and it would give her more independence.

What was more, she'd get married before too long, Emanuela decided, smiling to herself as she stood up with a light, gay motion and began to drift along the quay in the warm, briny dusk. Oh, for heaven's sake, not to a good-looking oaf like Gastone, and not to a nasty piece of work like Tiziana's husband, however much money he had in the bank. But to one of her childhood friends maybe – he'd have to be a Venetian and they'd have to live here, she wasn't going to the mainland. A man who was doing reasonably well in his profession or his business. A man who'd like it that she kept up her contacts in the music world, who'd like it that she contributed to their income by working at the singing school. With any luck, children would be born, she thought happily, passing in amused review several old friends with whom she'd romped when they were all ten, or with whom she'd kissed and cuddled when they were fifteen, as baffled as ever by the way men and women caught fire with sensuality and tenderness, but deciding effortlessly that a by and large cheerful marriage was far from an impossibility. You just had to have sensible expectations as well as being romantic, and you had to work hard at things.

Emanuela dimpled, because she'd suddenly imagined how she might bump into Hugh Thurne after, say, a dozen years, perhaps in somebody's house, or perhaps she'd be walking along a dim portico and suddenly he'd be the figure coming toward her. Of course, they might be a bit taken aback for a moment – but then their eyes would sparkle, at once they'd be old friends. She'd ask him whether that unfortunate wife of his had ever managed to liberate herself from him. He'd ask how she was. She'd tell him proudly about how little Ruggiero and Annalisa (she had already chosen their names) were starting to enjoy music, how her husband and she were already choosing which ballets to take them to first.

And in the meantime, what now? she wondered, sauntering on in the nightfall, listening to the gulls. What now, with all these different dreams in her head? – or had they been there before?

Oh, this summer she wasn't going to change, she decided or she realised, but with none of her nervous irritability of recent weeks, robustly entertained by how well she knew herself. Summer was the time for indolence and for pleasure with old acquaintances and new, for revels in the Lido's ballrooms that went on all night and spilled out onto the moonlit beaches that smelled of the sea. It was already irresistible, it would be her last time of absolute freedom and not giving a damn, she thought, raising her finger-tips to her necklace and at once laughing softly to herself, because it was one of those in the Tiepolo style that she'd been rather going in for this year, worn high on her throat like a choker.

XXIII

'No, Francesco, I'm sorry, but I just can't get as steamed up as you about the crimes of our empire.' Stefano Moretta spoke distractedly, because they were really waiting to hear the answers to their fears that would shortly be offered by Dr Zanon, who had been summoned urgently and in the room above their heads was visiting his patient, and also because this month for the first time in his life he was not at his ease in his cousins' house. 'And if you'll forgive me, at least I've been out there doing the donkey work of our administration, so to a small extent I know what I'm talking about.'

Stefano did not have his two Venier cousins' good looks. But he was strongly built, his brown hair curled attractively however hard he rammed it down with a wetted brush, and his chubby face and his usually smiling brown eyes gave him an open, trusting air. He was sitting on the chaise-longue, one ankle across the other knee, and he was bumping his fist against his chin lightly and repeatedly.

'Oh, it's rough justice that we hand out, certainly it is,'

the visitor went on, quite unable to think why he was saying any of this, and glancing nervously toward the door to the staircase because for some reason his tense imagination had sensed that Gloria was coming into the room. 'But I don't think that we Italians do our colonising any more vilely than the other white races in Africa, and possibly we're more decent than some. For that matter, when you've witnessed what the Africans can get up to by way of justice and injustice when left to their own devices, and by way of the lack of much compassion ever, whether or not their victim is guilty of anything more serious than the mistake of being at their mercy . . .'

Remembering certain crimes and certain punishments, remembering evidence in the form of physical remains that he had come upon, Stefano swallowed. He took out his hand-kerchief, mopped his face and his neck, which suddenly had become wet and cold.

'No, what bothers me, Francesco, is the far more banal consideration that our colonies are run at a loss. Though of course, if what you're suggesting is that all we Europeans ought to recognise the error of our ways and pull out of Africa, I dare say I'd agree with you. But how could we organise that? France, England, Belgium, Spain and Portugal, Germany until this year when we've been dividing up the spoils . . . We're all in there, or nearly all of us – just think of the vested interests, the commercial hopes, the strategic jostling! But it's not the slightest bit glamorous, what we do – that's only the government in Rome talking things up. Where I was, month after month it was one stupid difficulty after another. Problems with irrigation, with tribal squabbling, with corruption and pilfering.'

The sun had been shut out of the lower *sala* all day and no lamps were lit. The pieces of furniture were shadowy mounds, the picture frames had lost their lustre.

'Oh, come off it, my dear fellow.' Lounging to his feet in the dimness, Francesco chuckled. 'When it comes to venality on a scale that befits a gentleman, when it comes to thefts committed with balance sheets and signatures, our own educated classes could teach your poor black pilferers a thing or two.' Standing beside an ebony and gilt table, he picked up a glass jug and swirled it, making a sloshing, chinking sound. 'Would you like some more of this lemon juice? No? There's a little left. Melted ice, chiefly. What do you reckon, can we risk hauling the awnings up? I heard the bells ringing six o'clock, it must be getting a bit cooler out there.'

Following Gloria's brother toward the windows, with an effort of will Stefano made himself be as amused and as self-deprecating as he usually was quite naturally. 'Of course, I probably *will* get around to agreeing with this anti-imperialism of yours. In my experience, I generally manage to think the right thing in the end. It's just that I always have to think a whole lot of wrong things first. Listen, you'll come out to La Badia one weekend before long, won't you, and tramp over some of my mud and dust with me, and give me lots of good advice about crops and livestock?'

Already raising the first of the long, dark blue awnings, Francesco grinned. 'I'd love to. Especially now that I've remembered that arbour of yours where we can eat our lunch.

189

Only watch out, the weekend after that I'll probably march you off to our office here, lock you in with a few armfuls of my father's files about lawsuits that have been dragging on for years, and only let you out after you've briefed me.'

As cords were pulled and then belayed onto their tiny brass cleats, as pulleys rattled lightly and awning rods tapped against window-frames, the July afternoon filled arch after arch with hot, luminous blue. Suddenly sunlight reflected up off the water was wavering on the dark brown beams at the Grand Canal end of the long room. Farther back, the new brilliance brought out the upholstered chairs' faded crimsons and yellows, glinted on a cabinet's handles, gave each of the side doors one pale slope to its pediment.

Stefano Moretta leaned on the balustrade above the glinting water beside Francesco. Unfortunately, the sight of his native city immediately reminded him of how straightforward and how rich in promise the future had appeared when he'd been sweltering in a government office in Mogadishu, and how damned complicated everything had turned out to be when he'd come home and tried to persuade the future actually to begin.

How he'd longed for all this! He'd dreamed of Italy, he'd dreamed of working hard at farming so that he could be prosperous and he could spread prosperity, like an idiot he'd dreamed of Gloria, or maybe not like an idiot. And now here he stood beside her brother at their windows over the Grand Canal; in other words he was in exactly the sort of circumstances that on the shores of that romantic, depressing Indian Ocean he'd yearned for, and there were all these difficulties.

Cottages needed to be repaired, outhouses needed to be repaired, not to mention the ruinous condition of the villa itself. Farm implements that had been in use since the previous century must be replaced by modern machinery if he was ever to achieve an annual profit. On the one hand, it seemed madness to borrow capital until he could be reasonably confident that he was making enough money to start to pay the loan back. On the other hand, when with trepidation he'd resolved that he'd be compelled to go into debt in order to make his modest estate even begin to be economically viable, bankers who professed themselves old schoolfriends of his father had assured him mournfully that they'd be obliged to charge him the most alarming rates of interest.

Worst of all, as soon as this English fellow Robert had turned up ten days ago, it had been dismayingly plain that before Gloria had only been happy to eat ice-cream in a café with him or go boating with him because he was a cousin she'd always got on well with, and that was all he'd ever be. Or was he wrong about that? It wasn't *possible* that he'd been completely deluded, there *had* been a tenderness between Gloria and him all last month. Those black eyes of hers had given him lingering glimmers that he would never forget. And even today, when he'd come down to Venice by train to ask after her father, it had really been in the hope of seeing her.

Oh God, oh God, *why* was he such a fool? He'd put on his newish summer suit, he'd remembered to polish his shoes. He was even wearing his favourite blue and yellow bow-tie, one that his father had passed on to him and that he liked for that reason, one that was a bit of a talisman and might bring him luck. Well, so Gloria was perfectly capable of flirting with him in June and flirting with somebody else in July, of course she was, why shouldn't she be? Oh but why, *why*? No, the thing was to take a much more sanguine view. She'd be bored with this fellow Robert before the summer was over. For heaven's sake, she'd only just turned sixteen! Yes, but if last month she'd really been becoming keen on him, she wouldn't from one week to the next have started taking Robert out in her boat what sounded like every day.

There must have been a hatch of midges quite low over the water, because swifts had hurtled down and were swooping east and west and up and around before the eyes of the two young men, each leaning with his shoulder against a column. Across the tideway at San Stae, a one-time soldier hobbled on crutches to the church door and lowered himself to the steps. Neighbours started to go in for evening mass.

Instinctively casting around for something to feel cheerful about, Stefano had instead remembered an occasion on the Somali coast, when the principles of enlightened Christian administration had required a black wretch to be given fifty lashes, which was fortunate for him, because a couple of other fellows estimated to have been more deeply involved in the same crime had a quarter of an hour before been hanged. He'd remembered how, in order that the correct number of strokes should be administered, it had been necessary to continue the punishment for several minutes after the man's back had become flayed meat, the sergeant flogging him showing commendable steadiness, though afterward he'd got drunk.

Immediately after that, Stefano remembered an evening – he'd been up-country, in some hell-hole among the dry hills – when the principle of not interfering with local customs had required, in the view of his superiors, that they should not intervene when a native council decided, in accordance with their own principles, that a man should be impaled. Whenever life was particularly horrifying, there was always some damned moral principle behind it, you could rely on that – either the principle of progress, of modern European civilisation, or some other principle. He remembered how, after the man had been taken away to have this done to him, he'd stood at the side of a track near his bungalow, thankful that he was out of earshot, imagining the first few minutes of the punishment. He remembered how late that night he'd been unable not to walk near the place of execution. Near enough to hear that the victim was still screaming.

Frowning in his wretchedness, Stefano brought back how all through those three years he'd been buoyed up by the half-certainty that there'd always been something special about Gloria's and his friendship, how in his loneliest times his imagination had kept seeing his pretty girl cousin's sly, laughing eyes. And then, when he'd come home in May, she'd been almost a woman and she'd been bewitching. Oh, for pity's sake, of course she'd have a few boyfriends. But perhaps in time, if he was steady and she saw that, she'd find that her feeling for him was strengthening not diminishing.

Only last month, despite how ill her father was, it had been almost as if there'd been no sadness in the offing at all. One evening Francesco had said: 'I've discovered where our bat colony has shifted to. Would you like to come and have a look?'

His cousins had led him up to the top of this house. The three of them had gone ducking up the attic stair, then up the rickety wooden steps onto the roof terrace, the *altana*, where honeysuckle and jasmine rooted in vast terracotta pots straggled up dilapidated posts and trellises. Up there in the twilight, in the silence that was only ever broken by the winds and by church bells and by cats that wauled, Francesco had pointed to a tiny crack in a gully between two ridges of the roof.

They'd leaned their elbows on the rail, they'd waited. Soon there had been a faint scratching sound as the first bat crept toward the minute aperture. Then in an instant its gaunt black shape had gone flitting away into the gloaming. After a pause, they'd seen a second, a third. It had been good, lingering peacefully up there together on the sky-line, counting bats. In the end, they'd had a tally of thirty or more. And all the while he'd been thinking of how La Badia would be, after he had asked Gloria if she would marry him and she had said yes, when they would be walking there together, past the carp pond, through the orchard. He'd imagined how he'd tell her his plans for grubbing up the vineyard and planting a new one on a different slope, he'd imagined how she'd ask him why his proposed site would be better and he would explain. Happy dreaming, that was what was unforgivably stupid! Dreams about how, with their arms around one another, they'd go up to the abandoned third storey of the villa, which was in a frightful state of disrepair, but which they were going to have put to rights so they could live there in complete independence from his parents. Whereas what in fact would happen would be that in a few years she'd meet someone new, she'd fall in love, in a matter of months she'd be married and living in Rome or Milan or somewhere.

Dr Zanon must have left his patient by now; doubtless Valentina and he were conferring in another room. But Francesco wasn't talking nervously or glancing about, Stefano noticed admiringly. He was smoking a cigarette, watching the boats, apparently as calm as ever, though this summer since his father had been ill his old light-heartedness had gone, and he almost never started a conversation but just responded to what people said.

Stefano gave him a rueful smile. He said impulsively: 'Shall I tell you what a neurotic imbecile I am? I was here at these windows a few weeks ago with your mother and mine. They were joking that, since you'd become so disgracefully hand-some, all they had to do was to stand you right here till the next young Philadelphia heiress drifted past in her gondola, and all the family's problems would be solved for the next hundred years at least. And – well, I told you this didn't redound to my credit. I immediately decided that what the two of them *really* meant was that they ought to stand Gloria at this window until the next millionaire came by.'

And Stefano blushed, because he hadn't meant to say all that – or perhaps he had, perhaps it was a relief to say too much, a relief not to have his cousin be in any doubt at all. Then he blushed more hotly, at the thought that perhaps it had merely been a pleasure to talk about himself, to be the centre of attention for a few seconds.

'Idiot,' Francesco replied equably, and went on lazily contemplating the Grand Canal. Then he swung around, because his mother had hurried in behind them.

XXIV

'He's gone!' Valentina exclaimed in a tired voice, meaning the doctor. 'He . . . Oh, darling boy. I don't know what to think any longer. I . . . He says . . .'

Francesco was already beside his mother and had put one arm around her. She stood utterly still, her grey face and her grey hair laid against his chest, for a minute not saying anything.

'It's all right, Mamma.' His voice was low and tranquil, was even amused. 'It's all right, whatever old Zanon has just been saying to you. And whether he's right about Papa or he's wrong, it's all right anyhow.' Francesco looked away, above his mother's head. He gave her shoulder a slight squeeze. 'You're doing marvellously. You're doing everything that you possibly could. Steady, you old darling. Steady does it.'

Valentina gently detached herself. She drew a deep breath.

'He says – now, let me get it right. What did he say? He says that your father did have a stroke a few hours ago, as we'd thought. It may have been the first, but perhaps it was the second. He says that Giacomo can be said to be recovering from this. His voice is faint, but he can talk now. However, he's extremely weak. Darling – Zanon made a point of having me understand that your father is very, *very* weak. He also said that it's extremely unlikely that he will not have another stroke eventually. And . . . You know, old Zanon and I have known each other for so many years. He said that – well . . . that in many ways, we should all be forgiven for hoping that, if he does have another stroke, next time it's a really bad one, a mercifully bad one.'

Francesco stood still, pressing his lips together firmly. Then in the quietness he said, 'Right,' gently. 'Well . . . It's been coming for a long time.'

With an effort, Valentina Venier made herself turn her attention for a minute from the dying to the living: to Gloria, whose romantic firework show, her mother reminded herself, had only lately begun and was likely to produce a good few bangs and flashes in the next years; to Francesco who'd become so grown-up, who could be depended upon to say the right thing, but who this year had stopped ever initiating a conversation about himself with her. And Gloria kept joking that she'd been strewing her prettiest friends at her brother's feet and draping them around his neck, but no luck so far.

Most immediately of all, here was Stefano, to whom she'd been devoted all his life, whose mother and father she'd loved all her life. Honestly – young people's ability to tear each other to tatters! So right this minute, the poor lad must be bundled off back to the mainland and to Asolo before worse occurred.

Valentina glanced down the Rialto reach of the Grand Canal and realised that it was too late. Sitting side by side in the Ca' Zante gondola, Violet Mancroft and Hugh Thurne were approaching the house. In five minutes they'd be here, wanting to know how Giacomo was today, hoping that they might see him for half an hour, which certainly this evening would be out of the question. And a short way behind them, in the blue and grey *sandolo*, Gloria and Robert were both standing up for some reason, making the little skiff wobble even on the calmest of evenings.

One of them was taking over the oar from the other, the girl's mother made out – and no doubt they were giggling, and no doubt these were blissful opportunities for touches.

She turned back into the *sala*, for an instant seeing once more a dance in this room back in the early nineties when Giacomo had first taken her hand and put his other arm around her waist for a waltz. Then that lost time and its colours and its music thinned to shreds like a mist when a breeze gets up.

Stefano, standing beside her, said with resolute heartiness: 'Well, I must go, or I'll miss my train.'

Left in solitude for a few minutes while Francesco went downstairs to see his cousin off and to welcome Hugh Thurne and the Mancrofts, Valentina sank into a chair thankfully. Once more the separation that Giacomo and she had been steeling themselves for had approached nearer, once more it had hesitated, but their goodbye must be close now. At the same time, she had recalled a stormy night last winter and Hugh standing by the mantelpiece talking about the war as an immense evil that had been committed, an evil that could never be undone and never be atoned for, that was going to reverberate through the survivors' lives until they died.

There was Robert, cheerfully messing about on the water with Gloria below her windows, who would carry his father's death within him and be harmed by it for the rest of his days. And now these deaths in peacetime too, she thought. Now her Francesco and her Gloria were going to lose their father. Gloria especially, who'd been out with the Mancrofts since morning and didn't yet know about Giacomo's stroke, Gloria who was about to have her merriment dispelled – she was so young still! Oh, Hugh was wretchedly right, of course he was, the effects of the war weren't going to die away till those who'd been children when it was fought had died. But in the lulls of peace between the wars people had to live all they could, she suddenly resolved with tired, dogged passion. Carrying their grief and their damage, men and women and children had to summon all the love and the gaiety they could, even if often it didn't come all that naturally.

Valentina stood up abruptly and crossed to the windows, thinking of how, no doubt ever since the civilisations on the Euphrates and on the Nile, after all the wars people had decided that everything was going to be better, but thinking too that this was a serviceable folly. And now, in this partic-ular lull of peace when with a spot of luck she herself might hope to stay alive, in these next ten or conceivably twenty or more years when she might hope to be a small force for good in a handful of people's destinies. What psychological changes was she going to get glimpses of in her son and her daughter that Giacomo would never know about, what happinesses and unhappinesses? Was she going to be any good at backing up Francesco and Gloria, helping them? – without Giacomo at her side, but as he'd wish her to, for love of him as well as for love of them. Upstairs he was still alive, but it wasn't awful to start to think of him as almost beginning to be in her memory, she decided a little awkwardly but firmly, sadly. As their parting came closer, she *had* to brace herself for it more and more.

She looked out. Vertically beneath her, bare-headed Francesco was standing on the jetty as the Ca' Zante boat came alongside. Hugh was wearing a Panama hat, and Violet had a straw concoction with a light blue riband that looked encouragingly light-hearted. Fifty paces off, Robert was in charge of the skiff's oar. Sitting on the thwart, Gloria was in peals of laughter at how inexpertly he rowed or at something else.

A grey, podgy vixen standing guard over my three-quarters-grown cubs, Valentina thought, that's who I've become.

XXV

The effects upon Hugh of his conversation with Violet Mancroft late that Easter night in the library at Ca' Zante had been manifold, had astonished and amused him as well as making him fear for a return of his depression, and had begun at once.

While he was still in Venice, he made a point of never being alone with her again, although one morning he took his godson by motor launch to visit the basilica on the island of Murano, bringing him back to Venice in time for lunch, and on another occasion they packed a picnic in a knapsack and had their launch take them farther north across the lagoon to Torcello. With Violet, he never returned to the question of whether she would accept his offer of the top floor of his house, merely leaving her, when he set off for France and England, a note written on one side of a sheet of paper to say that she would give him great pleasure if she cared to take him up on this.

In London, Hugh conducted a conversation with his wife

utterly different from the one he had planned. In a manner so impeccable that it would have delighted any of his old friends, he said that he'd always reckoned divorces were a ghastly business, especially for the children of the self-regarding pair, but he fully acknowledged that he'd been an abysmal husband, so if she wished to she might tell her lawyers that he would make no effort to defend himself, though he couldn't help hoping that on reflection she would decide not to push ahead with this. When his boys came home for their half-term holiday, he behaved like the most affectionate and cheerful of fathers and husbands, immediately after which he went to stay at his club, so as not to be in his wife's way, and from which he could easily walk to the Foreign Office. A few weeks later he was back in Paris, fairly confident that Elizabeth's love affair with Bill Knox was precisely that, a love affair, just as his own with Emanuela Zuccarelli had been, and that when the brigadier was posted back to his own country she would remain in England.

Hugh Thurne behaved in all these ways, which seemed to him perfectly coherent as well as making him smile at himself, because day and night in his mind he was talking to Violet, asking her about her childhood, about her marriage to Philip, about how she was now, telling her about himself. He wanted to do all his remembering from now on with her rather than with other people or alone. He wanted to emerge from the shadow of the war alongside her, it didn't matter in what sort of contact with her, but in touch in one manner or another.

As soon as he returned to Venice for his summer sojourn,

a surprising number of people appeared to feel under an obligation to hint to him that during the months he'd been away Emanuela had been up to all sorts of high jinks. This made him feel a lot better, because it meant that she'd understood too. When Marcella Zancana, who lived around the corner from Ca' Zante and whom he seemed to knock up against on the quay three times in his first two days back, took the opportunity of mentioning the celebrated conductor Della Rovere, Hugh at once guessed that she'd been put up to this by Valentina Venier and he was delighted that Valentina and he were already allies. Also he was amused, because he'd met Della Rovere a few times in people's drawing-rooms, and he knew him too as a man who'd frequented the House of Masks on an island at a not inconvenient distance from St Mark's. The House of Masks was one of the most luxurious and expensive houses of pleasure in the Old World, quite on a par with the most sumptuous establishments in the capital cities, and he himself as well as Della Rovere had been in the habit of occasionally telling his gondoliers to convey him there after dinner parties, in the years before his intoxication with Emanuela Zuccarelli had caused him to abandon that distraction.

And all this time, on account of how wrong he'd been about Elizabeth in his thirties and about Emanuela in his forties, on account of how obtuse he'd been all his life whenever a smidgin of self-knowledge had been called for, Hugh Thurne could feel his depression gathering in the distance, like a tide that far out at sea was turning and was about to come flooding in. After all his idealising of Emanuela, his letting his mind fashion her in the image it found enchanting merely in order that his sensual enjoyment of her should have some sort of justification; after all his dreams about a future with her ... What had occurred? It had been like walking past a bonfire, so naturally for a minute your nose and your eyes were full of woodsmoke – but then you walked on and you saw again. Yes, but this meant that, just as he had repeatedly deluded himself and others, quite likely he was deluding himself now – and it would be unforgivable to delude Violet.

How often did you have to be fraudulent before you realised that you were essentially fraudulent? Well, there was an answer to that, an answer that he returned to ceaselessly and each time couldn't help rediscovering was brilliant. Violet didn't need to know the slightest thing about what he felt for her. Some sort of lack of unhappiness in time to come would only be remotely feasible, certainly for him and he hoped for her, if she suspected little or nothing for many years, possibly for ever.

There remained the problem of Emanuela, to whom he undoubtedly owed ... Well, what did he owe her? Nothing? The good taste not to insist on any foolish talk when all was plain?

He by his neglect of her and she by her starting a fling with Amedeo Della Rovere had irrevocably put their relations back into the category of light-hearted liaisons in which they had been initiated and in which it might have been better to let them exhaust their delectable, commonplace impulse. And the old, worldly maxim remained as true as ever: in these matters you should never apologise and you should never explain.

Yes, yes . . . But when he remembered some of their evenings drifting through the backwaters on their way to discover a ceiling that Tiepolo had painted, when he remembered her arrivals at his water-gate on spring nights – there'd been real tenderness, there'd been real gaiety and fellow-feeling. He didn't think he wanted to pretend none of that had occurred. How they'd been that last time he'd seen her; the amusement and the liking in her eyes when she'd said – what was it she'd said? – standing by the theatre in her navy blue mackintosh, looking damnably ravishing as usual. 'Tell me when you're next free. Oh, and . . . Last night was wonderful.' Something like that.

Explaining was for bores, unquestionably – but he wanted to see her, he wanted to say goodbye, he wanted to know that things were on the level between him and her. That day when he'd been waiting for her in the garden of this house, that afternoon when he'd been pacing to and fro on the gravel path and the light had been fantastic, before that confusing letter from London had arrived and made him even sillier than he generally was . . . He remembered thinking then that, when the time came for Emanuela and him to go their different ways, which it was bound to before long, they'd each know how to say goodbye with scarcely diminished liking, with amusement, above all without regret either for what had been or for what was now going to be.

Well aware of how muddled his reasoning was, but acting on an instinct he felt was sound, Hugh waited until Violet and Robert had gone to Florence for a week. Then he sent Emanuela a few lines saying that he was back in town and asking whether she would like to come and see him.

This was the sweltering day of the cloudburst when the Ca' Zante gondola with Emanuela on board and rowed by Gastone took shelter beneath a bridge not far from Campo dei Mori. After the rain, Hugh remembered that although the brief downpour had been just what the languishing garden needed, up in the loggia Violet's two lemon trees in their tubs would still be dry. That was why he was at the top of the house when Emanuela arrived. And he was still standing between the pillars of the loggia with a watering-can in his hand when he saw her striding away across the little square.

Both his eyebrows went up. He said, 'Good heavens!' out loud. Then he smiled, because he'd thought: Well, well, I wonder what *her* views on explaining are, or whether I'll ever be honoured with a version that's – oh, amused and amusing.

Suddenly having nothing particular to do, he finished giving the lemon trees a thorough drenching and went downstairs. Intrigued, so that his wish to see Emanuela in the next few days felt more urgent, he remembered that the Veniers had sent word that at the Madonna dell'Orto on Sunday the war memorial was to be unveiled and there would be a special mass for the dead of that parish, among them poor Donatella's young husband. Naturally since his stroke Giacomo would not even be able to hobble downstairs leaning on somebody's arm and be taken to the ceremony in the gondola, but the rest of the family would be there.

Like all of those highish in the armed forces, in the Church, in politics and in government service, Hugh Thurne since the previous winter had been present at the dedication of a lot of memorials and a lot of war cemeteries, and in the months and years to come he would be present at many more. He had no official reason to be at the occasion at the Madonna dell'Orto, and he hadn't even got around to deciding whether he'd go or not, but now he decided that he would. Emanuela's flat was less than a hundred yards from the church, all her neighbours would attend and so almost certainly would she.

XXVI

Violet and her son, returned to Venice, were about to set off for the Madonna dell'Orto in the Ca' Zante boat, but Hugh decided he would cross the city on foot. He felt like stretching his legs, and he was going to see the Mancrofts anyway, after the ceremony, at lunch in the Venier house. Above all, he had woken up that morning already thinking happily about Violet; he wanted to go on thinking about her and about the ideas and feelings she seemed spontaneously to cause to fountain in his consciousness, and this could be done just as well, or perhaps even more freely and delightfully, when he was not in her company. He hadn't taken a decision never to see her of his own volition, but only when it occurred in the everyday course of things; it was an instinct he followed quite naturally.

Hugh Thurne walked slowly so as not to get into a sweat, keeping in the shade of the buildings so far as was possible, and grumbling good-temperedly to himself about the need for a dark suit and a black hat in this weather.

What if Violet had gone at Easter to Provence, where he knew she had old friends with a country house? What if they had offered her a flat in their place and she'd accepted, or if she'd found a pretty cottage near by that took her fancy? But she hadn't gone to the South of France, he reminded himself blithely. She'd come here to Venice, knowing that he was at the other end of the Grand Canal to Giacomo and Valentina, and after wavering for a bit she'd accepted his offer of the top floor of his house.

So now ... Well, one thing was that when Robert went up to Trinity at the end of the summer, he'd find an opportunity after a month or so to take the lad out to lunch, find out how he was settling in, see if there was any help or advice that might usefully be offered. In due course, too, he must see about getting his godson elected to a club, either his own or the one that had been Philip's, whichever Robert thought he'd plump for. And the marvellous thing would be that, while the two of them were wielding their knives and forks at a table in Cambridge or in London, at the back of his mind he'd know that Violet was here in Venice, she was coming and going from the street door of the house or from the canal gate, free to begin to recover a little in time. What was more, Philip Mancroft would be amused by this situation. Oh, he'd tease him ruthlessly of course, and in years to come, when it would not be unkind, he'd tease Violet too. But he'd reckon that under the circumstances this was all right – better for her, perhaps, and for Robert, than other possibilities. How strange, this thinking of Philip as both a friend who'd never come back and also as a spirit who in some sense was still alive, was utterly real, who held opinions, who chuckled at things, who spoke in a voice he remembered from when they were both nineteen.

And if things had fallen out differently? If Philip had come home, put his uniform away in a box-room cupboard in mothballs, taken up his farming and his politics again? Oh, then he himself would probably have behaved idiotically with one or two more pretty women before he really did become too ancient for that sort of nonsense. Violet and Philip would have continued to invite him to Brack for shooting weekends in winter and to sail *Calypso* down the coast with them in summer, and they'd have continued to love one another. So what had been the catalyst, why had Violet's and his conversation in his library here that Easter night been far more intense than their old talks before the war? Death, and their reactions to death, simply.

Sauntering along a shady portico behind the Misericordia, Hugh smiled to himself, as he always did these days at the thought of the triangle of Violet and Philip and himself. How right it was, to put her up in his house and try to look after her a little; how right it felt, that essentially it didn't matter whether in future years this friendship was transmuted into a stronger attachment or it wasn't. *I am in love, you say; I do not think so, exactly.* Which of the poets was that? Where did it echo to him from? Well, for years she wasn't going to suspect anything, even if there was something to suspect, and after that she'd either say, 'Oh, for heaven's sake, Hugh, don't be ridiculous,' or she wouldn't. In the meanwhile, what good spirits he'd been in ever since spring! And how cheerfully virtuous he'd become! Something was up. And how disgracefully you could behave for years and years, and then suddenly and of course undeservedly be damned nearly happy.

She'd said that if he'd been around last autumn when the news came, he'd have been the person she would have turned to. 'God almighty, how I've missed you!' she'd said. (As he had regularly done since April, Hugh Thurne made himself smile at his own silliness by recalling her exact words.) 'Hugh, you'll keep a kind of vague eye on me, won't you?' That too, in her voice. 'I sort of promised him I'd turn to you. No, don't say anything. I know you will.'

Violet had come alight when he'd imagined other evenings on which they'd remember their old world from before the war that seemed so annihilated now, when he'd imagined what living things the stories they told might seem to be. Emerging from the portico into the blaze of the morning heat (the ceremony was due to begin at eleven o'clock), happily dreaming of future evenings when she and he would bring things back, Hugh suddenly comprehended something, or he thought he did. The past wasn't dead; the past was that which was already alive – it was as straightforward as that! In any sense except the laughably superficial, it struck him now, time was never irrevocably lost. Centuries-ago time, minutes-ago time; time that had momentarily seemed to be his, momentarily seemed to be other people's (and perhaps this distinction wasn't of much account really) . . .

Time was all about him, only he'd never noticed – or rather, he hadn't understood before that this was time's way of being alive. These instants endlessly lapsing in your brain held it all, or held as much as your limited spirit happened to be capable of. Heavens – which particular brand of Asiatic sage was he turning into? To be open to time; to let time come ghosting in at your eyes and at your ears, see it, listen to it, think it. Lord, it was hot! Well, he'd be at the church in a couple of minutes. He'd try to work this out a bit more logically after the mass. No, he wouldn't, because the lunch party was going to be fun, as Valentina's lunches always had been and as they still were, despite Giacomo being so ill. He'd work out if any of these intimations stood up to scrutiny when he was walking home afterward, which he wouldn't do till it became cool.

Outside the Madonna dell'Orto, with its mediaeval statue of St Christopher over the door, the parish priest and a crowd from the neighbourhood had already gathered. Some of the city's dignitaries were there too: the mayor, the bishop, local politicians, the French and British consuls, both of whom approached Hugh to shake his hand.

Recollecting guiltily that he had come in the hope of seeing Emanuela Zuccarelli for a couple of minutes, he scanned the heads but she wasn't there. More people kept arriving, all looking sombre. The young knife-grinder propped his bicycle against a bollard and hobbled across to the white tablet of stone, which was the mournful addition to the west wall of the small square. It was a large tablet, to accommodate the dozens of names; a pair of wrought-iron sconces had been fixed into the masonry on either side of it, and this morning torches had been lit in them, the flames almost invisible in the brilliant air. Hugh noticed that the knife-grinder tried to stand as upright as he could and for that minute of devotion to lean on his crutch scarcely at all, before he turned and limped back into the crowd. Other survivors more vilely crippled were present, who most days crouched in supplication at this or neighbouring church doors. Like the other men who had fought, these young mendicants had put on the uniforms in which they had served, trouser legs and tunic sleeves pinned up where necessary.

Men, women and children stepped forward to look closely at the memorial, to check that their lost ones had not, by some error of the military authorities, been omitted from the roll of those killed for Italy, or that their names had not been misspelled. And they stepped closer and dwelt on the names as a telling over of sorrow yet again, Hugh thought; it was yet another minute in the long grieving that was the last act of love defeated by war. Many of the women were in tears. Some of the older men, whose boys had been killed, blew their noses into handkerchiefs, which they then folded and discreetly touched to their eyes.

Holding his hat in his hand as he waited for the ceremony to begin, Hugh Thurne felt the stupefying high summer sun on his head. A barge laden with rubble was rowed slowly past, the men straining and sweating. Hearing ripples flop against the quay, he was suddenly oppressively aware of miles of warm lagoon stretching all around, that shallow half-sea rotting in its black pit. While here . . . The pity of it! These helpless people, who had been irrevocably harmed, who stood with dignity. Italy hadn't needed to go to war. (He remembered his own amused disgust at the time, though of course

Britain and France had been glad of an ally. He remembered chats with Giacomo Venier, who'd never quite been able to resist a grim delight in the chance of Italy at last defeating Austria.) The nation had not been threatened. It had been sheer, base political opportunism.

An old, dull anger and wretchedness stirring in him, Hugh recalled how right up until Rome had opted for the Allies and against the Central Powers they'd been haggling with both sides. Immediately after which, the rant about *la patria* had been set in motion and people had been duped. And now this, in every parish in the land. What was more, he couldn't help sourly noticing, they hadn't even bought Carrara marble for this memorial, but a softer stone. Fine for a lot of purposes no doubt; but for incised lettering . . . After a hundred years, how much of this undying glory the bishop would soon start holding forth about would remain?

The Mancrofts had arrived, and now the Venier household was descending the bridge. For a moment Hugh was caught by how grown-up the brother and sister looked, walking side by side, with their grave faces. Yes, Gloria too . . . In a black dress, in a black bonnet – she'd been turned into a figure of grief already. And it must be the first time in her life she'd been decked out in a veil. So this was what she was going to look like at her father's funeral.

Then Hugh frowned with compassion. Supported on either side by Valentina and by Elena, poor Donatella had clearly been broken anew by her agony. As she was helped forward to see her husband's name carved in stone, her whole frame trembled, her mouth was working pitifully and her eyes streamed. Hugh saw Valentina attempt to dry Donatella's tears, clearly not for the first time. He saw Gloria unobtrusively remove the sodden handkerchief from her mother's hand and substitute her own dry one. Then it seemed kinder not to watch.

The memorial had been dedicated, the bishop had pronounced his homily, the congregation were entering the huge, damp-streaked church for the commemorative mass. Wondering why Emanuela Zuccarelli had not come, Hugh was still lingering beneath St Christopher after everyone else had gone in, scanning the small square and the bridge over the canal, when she came hurrying around the corner.

Seeing him on his own by the big Gothic doorway, she wavered, but then she approached him, though more slowly.

How chaste she looked in mourning, he thought, her brilliant hair nearly occluded by black velvet and black gauze. Still, she stood close enough to him below the arch for him to breathe the sandalwood she'd always worn, and for him to see from the glimmer in her eyes that she still liked him just as he still liked her.

Feeling relieved and cheerful, Hugh said: 'I hoped I might see you here.'

'I ought to have been here a quarter of an hour ago. I *was* here a quarter of an hour ago, actually, but I saw you, so for some reason I decided instead to go for a stroll along the canal. These days, it rather appears that at the merest sight of you I take to my heels. I'm sorry about the other afternoon. So absurd of me. Or perhaps not so misguided as all that.'

Hugh waited, his eyes smiling at her.

'I was . . . After I came away from your garden, I did some mulling things over that I don't reckon did me any damage. I'm afraid it didn't occur to me to come back and see if you were still in the house. I was sauntering; I was thinking,' she said. 'Listen, the service is beginning. Shall we go in?'

XXVII

Violet Mancroft would have had to be still in her first grief not to take some pleasure in her eyrie at the top of Ca' Zante with its loggia and its lemon trees. It was a relief to her that Hugh did not appear to be conducting a particularly rackety existence any longer. His pitching up occasionally and then going away for months suited her. She rejoiced in the trouble he took over Robert, and in how Robert loved going with him to churches and islands.

Above all, after everything that she had lived through the year before, to Violet it felt good to busy herself with the practicalities of her new life in a new country, and having only five rooms to fuss over it was easy to have an effect. She bought counterpanes and cushions; she had armchairs re-covered. She had her books sent out from England in trunks, and after she had unpacked them, kneeling on the library floor and trying not to cry when she took out novels that Philip had given her, she completely reorganised the shelves, which led to surplus volumes having to be housed in bookcases in bedrooms and elsewhere.

In a hazy sort of manner, Violet knew that what she was doing was making a fortress for herself at the top of that house, a safe place that might as well also be comfortable and pretty, where she and her woundedness could start to come to terms with each other. But her instinct was scarcely to rationalise this at all, merely to get on with it – though at the back of her mind it was not unpleasing to know that Giacomo and Valentina Venier, and for that matter darling old Hugh too, were all in favour of what she was doing, were utterly on her side. So she fixed up her apartment with stoves for when the winter should come (having had this idea, Hugh had left the country without doing anything about it). She came to an agreement with a tradesman from around the corner who was going to supply her with paraffin, to be delivered in drums that must, please, not be so big that they couldn't be lugged up to the top of the house. She took to buying flowers every few days and putting them in vases, until it occurred to her that it would be more sensible, and might even be fun, to grow them in the garden.

So she wrote to Hugh, who by then was back in Paris for what turned out to be the last time as one of the negotiators at the Peace Conference. Of course she wouldn't dream of interfering with his trees and his arbours, she promised him – only come to think of it, what about their doing a bit of pruning later in the year if he felt like giving her a hand one day? But those ruins of flower-beds along the garden's walls, those stretches of dust heaped with years of fallen leaves and sprouted through by sickly weeds – what did he feel, might it be an idea to have a go at resurrecting them? Oh and by the way, the flycatchers in the nest they'd found had flown.

Violet bought a spade and a hoe, she bought a rake and a trowel and secateurs. She put on her oldest clothes, and worked early in the morning before it was hot and in the evening again when the shadows came. She never stopped thinking about Philip, but it was less ghastly when she was busy doing something straightforward, something that might even be of modest usefulness. She knew that he would want her to begin to make a new life for herself; that he'd consider this Venice set-up was fine; that then he might toss in some further remark to the effect that, if after a few years she felt like doing something else, well, why not? The trouble was, she knew in advance that this new life of hers was going to be a poor thing, because new life needed to be longed for to be any good, and what she desperately longed for was her old life that she couldn't have.

She knew that Philip would not want her to be distraught for too long. She could hear his voice. 'Oh, my poor darling – gently, gently. That's enough.' Something like that, he'd say. So, kneeling with her trowel in her hand she'd give a whimper, she'd mop her eyes with her sleeve, glance anxiously around because the housekeeper might be approaching with a message or a question. And luckily there were other things she could hear in Philip's voice that made her get to her feet, that made her shrug her shoulders, give a rueful, sick-hearted, lingering smile, and decide that she'd finished today's scrabbling about in the dirt, she was going to put her tools away and get cleaned up.

Philip in the drawing-room at Brack, lounging back in a chair with one of those Turkish cigarettes he loved, Philip with Hugh – oh, with Hugh of course, always. 'Listen, old lad, you diplomats practically never put yourselves in harm's way, but . . . Well, I'm off to Alexandria, and to God knows where after that, and none of us has a clue what it's going to be like out there.' Knowing Philip so well, loving him so truly, that was her besetting affliction and it was going to be until she died, Violet would think, as she rinsed her muddy hands under the garden standpipe, unable not to go on hearing the sorts of things he'd said. 'But if I'm one of those who don't make it home again . . . You'll do what you can for Robbie, Hugh, I know you will. But . . . Oh, for God's sake, old fellow, look at me a bit less quizzically, can't you? May I – oh, I don't mean in any sense leave you Violet in my will. But you and she took a terrific shine to one another the very first evening I introduced you, and you've been in cahoots ever since, and you both have flickerings of good sense. You might find that you could back each other up, that life was less dreary when you weren't too far apart.' Even before Philip was killed, back in the war years when all her heart's strength had gone into not showing how afraid she was, she'd been wryly convinced by that echo in her head and by variations on it. Last summer when on the Brack estate the harvest had been in full swing, that day when Hugh had come over and at the lunch table she'd read him her latest letter from Mesopotamia, for a long minute while he was talking to Robbie she'd looked at him and she'd bitten her lip till it bled.

As soon as Violet had moved into Ca' Zante, Giacomo and Valentina had begun to invite her back to their house for lunch or for dinner at least once a fortnight. She loved these occasions, because of how protected, even cherished those two made her feel, apparently quite effortlessly. Because of the unbothered, affectionate way in which they talked about Philip or they didn't talk about him. And because the coming and going between these two houses nearly at either end of the Grand Canal seemed to her in her forlornness a possible beginning, a structural line on which warm-heartedness in the future might be built . . . Especially after London, where even six months after Philip's death she'd had the impression that a lot of her so-called friends would hardly ever mention him again, were only wondering when she'd have an affair or wondering which poor fellow she'd end up snaffling second time around.

Then Robert returned to Venice in July. Every day, it at once appeared, and sometimes twice a day, once after breakfast and then again in the evening, either he'd set off to the Venier house from where he would embark in the *sandolo* with his new friends (his new friends, as his mother knew, nine times out of ten meaning Gloria and no one else), or the young lady would appear below the facade of Ca' Zante, standing in the stern of her skiff, sculling with one hand on her oar, her left or her right indifferently. Whichever window he'd been watching from, Robert would go tumbling down the staircase. A minute later, he'd be on the jetty, and Gloria would be bringing her little boat alongside.

Violet was relieved that Gloria's parents were so liberal,

were so modern, when it came to smiling on this excessively romantic gallivanting. She absolutely understood why Francesco usually had more amusing things to do with his free evenings than to go dawdling into backwaters with Gloria and Robert, and she admired him, and she was sorry for him, for spending his summer vacation in an office.

When Robert took his lunch with his Venier godfather's family, she liked to imagine him there. She hoped that for him too, as for she herself in her a lot less vernal way, this toing and froing along this waterway between these two houses might begin a little to replace some of the cheerful security that in England he had lost – all that way of life that Philip and she had taken care over for him, that from one autumn day to the next hadn't been there any more.

When she was invited, or rather when she was practically commanded, to give her son and Gloria lunch in her house, she berated herself for the trouble she caused the housekeeper and herself to go to, and she wondered at the delight she took in the merriment and the shyness and the sea air those two brought into the dining-room. She worried how long this sort of enamouredness between two young people might continue, in old-fashioned Catholic Italy, before it was assumed that the engagement must be made official, and she recollected thankfully that at least she knew Valentina well enough to ask her a straight question. She worried about what effects being in love with a girl in Venice might have on Robert when he was at Cambridge, what effects on how happy he was, on how well he did – always supposing that Gloria and he didn't have some frightful coming to grief next week, or this minute were not causing one another tears of despair a few canals away.

Today after the commemorative mass at the Madonna dell'Orto, when they all came out of the church again into the square, when some members of the congregation went once more to stand before the new tablet on the wall, and others got into boats or began to walk off, all Violet's attention was focused on Valentina.

For the last two months, since Giacomo had been practically confined to his rattan chair, whenever she had gone to that house for lunch, Valentina and she had drawn up a little folding mahogany table near where he sat by his windows in the upper *sala*. But six of them could not do that, so on this occasion they would have to be in the dining-room, which was next door to the *sala* on the first floor, with the kitchen behind it. When they all returned to the house, it would be utterly unreasonable to expect anything from Elena other than that she should remain with her cousin in the bedroom that had been made over to her (and where, as Valentina had remarked, poor Donatella would almost certainly be established for the next half-century or thereabouts until she died); so the family and their guests were going to have to set to work in the kitchen, and Violet had already suggested to Robert that he might lend a hand laying the table.

Since Giacomo's stroke, he had never been left alone in the house. This morning an exception had been made, because of the importance of this war memorial to all their neighbourhood and above all to Donatella. Naturally he would be perfectly all right, drowsing against his cushions in his big, quiet house with all its awnings down. But even so, it must be a good hour and a half, perhaps two hours, since he'd been left, and Violet knew that Valentina was longing to get back to him. Well, she thought, it's no distance from here. Those of us who go by gondola (and Donatella must certainly have a place in one of them), or those who volunteer to walk – whether you slip along the canal by the red-brick wall of the nunnery garden, or you cross the bridge at Santa Fosca by the oar-maker's workshop . . . in ten minutes we'll all be there.

Throughout the summer, Violet Mancroft's old affection for Valentina Venier had been riveted onto the fact that the fate that had befallen herself last year was about to strike the other woman, what had been done to Robert was about to be done to Francesco and Gloria.

XXVIII

Violet went up the two flights of stone stairs beside Valentina, who deliberately was not hurrying. At the far end of the long, shadowy room, framed between two pale columns of *pietra d'Istria*, against a backdrop of dark blue canvas and the vertical slashes of pale brilliance where each slanted awning didn't quite meet the next, there Giacomo sat, his legs in his grey trousers stretched out and his shoes on the rattan foot-rest, his head lolled back.

He was so still that Violet's heart gave a jolt, she fell a step behind Valentina as they approached. No, he's alive, she thought, as Valentina sat down in her accustomed place opposite her husband, and leaned forward to lay her hand on his knee, and he opened his eyes. He's all right still – oh, thank the Lord! – though he seems a lot weaker than he was even ten days ago. How silly I am! And there's his stick with its silver knob propped against the stone where he can reach it, only these days it isn't of much service to him any more, Violet thought, standing a pace or two back from Valentina who was still leaning forward, who hadn't shifted either her hand or her gaze, who was waiting for Giacomo's depleted spirit to come a little more emphatically toward her before she spoke to him.

Here on his table are his lamp for when twilight comes, and a couple of books, Violet went on noticing nervously. (The cause of her commingled fascination and dread and compassion was that the approach of this death was so utterly different from how the approach of Philip's death had been; but this was so immense and was so immanent within her that she scarcely realised that it was why this minute she was so rattled.) Here are Giacomo's spectacles, and a little bottle with a stopper that I suppose quite likely has morphine in it, and a tiny flask of eau-de-Cologne, and the brass bell they gave him so he could ring it if he wanted something when no one was beside him . . . Why am I bothering about these things? He's still Giacomo – his eyes are gleaming, and look at that peacockish silk handkerchief just allowed to peep out of the breast pocket of his coat. A black coat, of course, even in these August dog days. What is Valentina saying?

'Darling, we're home again. And it wasn't so dreadful as it might have been, all things considered. Francesco and Gloria were wonderful. Now, we're all about to have some lunch. There's *pasta e fagioli*, which I thought you might manage a little bowl of, perhaps. After that we're having . . . Well, the fishmonger at San Leonardo was as convincing as ever, so we've got a quantity of *branzino* that I hope the younger generation are going to be hungry enough to demolish. I know you won't feel up to broth and then fish, just tell me which you'd prefer. What about half a *branzino*, say, if I filleted it for you? Oh, and Hugh is here, and he'd love to see you, if you feel up to it.'

'*Branzino*, please. Thank you. And I'd like to see Hugh.'

'I'll go!' exclaimed Violet. 'You stay with him, darling.'

Branzino, she thought, starting off toward the kitchen, that's sea bass, isn't it? – or sea bream, something like that. My Italian is getting better, but it isn't brilliant. My Italian is terrific when I don't have to say anything, when I can just listen and understand three-quarters of it and then be distracted. So this is how it is going to be: Valentina will be here, and I'll be on the other side of the city, and I'll try to be a strength to her as she's tried to be a strength to me and no doubt will go on being a strength to me. Who knows – perhaps scooping up Robbie and me and being enormously kind to us has even helped her? Perhaps it's been a distraction from being afraid for Giacomo and from worrying about their children. Perhaps it's been a modest, good thing she could get on with, rather like my deciding that every shelf in the library must be reorganised and the bedroom bookcases must be crammed. Rather like my rolling up my sleeves and plodding about with armfuls of books all on my own those hot afternoons in the shuttered rooms when all I ever heard were the bells at the end of the hour.

Well, we wretched widow women mustn't only try to sustain one another as best we may, there's more to it than that. (Violet was listening to her leather soles and high heels pitter-pattering down the staircase.) What was it Valentina said the other evening? Something about how she *refused* to

231

be only down-hearted and nothing else. In a sense she was already grieving for Giacomo, she said. She was beginning to grieve for their love, their marriage, their myriad moments together, which was reaching its twilight when only she, only memory would be left. But she was also going to come to life again in a small way, after however long that took, or at any rate she was going to try to. Well, she's right, Violet thought, entering the dining-room where Robert and Gloria were preparing for the lunch party. How awkward they became with one another as soon as she appeared in the doorway! And how delightful to have one's china and silver and glass laid out by a boy and a girl in love!

In the kitchen, Francesco was standing by the range, his thoughts clearly far away, giving the big simmering pot of *pasta e fagioli* an occasional stir with a wooden ladle, with the air of a young man who was not a cook but whose mother had asked him to do this.

Impulsively Violet put her arm around him and gave him a quick hug. 'Well done!' she said. Then she swung her gaze about the kitchen to see what she might usefully do. The fish had been gutted and rinsed, they were ready to go on the range. Judging by the delicious smell, potatoes with rose-mary and garlic were already roasting. Aubergines had been sliced, but not yet . . . Here was Hugh.

'Giacomo would love to see you,' she said. 'And lunch won't be for a few more minutes.'

As soon as Hugh had said, 'Oh good,' and swung on his heels, Violet forgot about the aubergines. She sauntered through into the lower *sala* where she was alone, taking out her cigarette case and her holder, her ideas of a few minutes before still looming up, so that she didn't even smile at how she'd been so keen that everybody should lend a hand, and here she was, the only person not helping at all.

For a moment she was tempted to smoke her cigarette looking out over the Grand Canal, but then she remembered that, at this time of the year and at this hour, on the facade of a house that faced south the heat and light would be intolerable. Better the awnings, better this dusk! Her silver holder in her right hand, she sauntered through the furniture as far as a gilt mirror that hung on one wall. She stood there, surveying herself in the dim glass, her left hand cupping her right elbow, her teeth just catching her lower lip.

Yes, this is how it's going to be, she thought. I'll be down on my hands and knees in the walled garden where the fountain dribbles (we might get that repaired), where all summer the leaf-mould has a tang of cats' piss but we're going to try to have the air smell of roses too, not only of cats and of the stagnant canal on the other side of the wall. Suddenly I'll sit back on my heels, I'll tilt up my head so I can see through the leaves to the evening sky, and my mind will be so brimming with the past, will be so brimful of stories that I won't know what to do. Sometimes Valentina will have come to be with me, sometimes she won't. There'll be times when we'll remember, when we'll imagine what may be to come, when we'll be quiet. Or Hugh will be there . . .

Because undoubtedly the occasion would be different with Hugh Thurne rather than Valentina Venier at her side (she might not be on her knees in the mould *all* the time), or

233

perhaps because her minute of self-contemplation had been satisfactory, Violet posed sidelong so she might better admire the line of her thigh and her hip in her slim black skirt, pouting as she puffed her cigarette.

A soft morning in autumn, perhaps, and Hugh and I will prune the arbours that have been allowed to straggle for years, she decided. We'll tidy up the medlar and the quince a little, we may even try to make some sense of the pomegranate that honestly is more of a thicket than a tree. Then at lunch on the iron table under the wisteria, or that evening when we've had our baths and made ourselves more or less presentable for dinner, or maybe not until late at night, he and I will talk. And it will be as he said it would be: our story-telling won't be all futile and it won't be all sad.

A couple of minutes later, coming into the upper *sala* with a bottle of Tocai and two glasses for the talkers, Violet saw Hugh sitting where Valentina had sat, leaning forward as she had done so that he could hear Giacomo's faint voice, his long legs bent, his elbows on his knees. 'Yes,' he was saying. 'But . . .'

She approached; she poured them each a glass of wine and received their smiles and their thanks; she gave them the good news that lunch was nearly ready. And then she lingered, because she'd caught a few words – it was the sort of conversation she remembered both of them having with Philip countless times.

'Half your colonies aren't worth having, and even those that make commercial sense – your Malay States, Hong Kong, Singapore . . . Or paramount political and strategic . . . India . . .' Giacomo's voice, which had used to be such a robust rumble, was scarcely audible and he kept stopping, but he knew what he wanted to say. 'With your fleets and armies . . . fight two wars in . . . two hemispheres at the same time? I mean . . . And the Mediterranean, Alexandria, Malta . . . Overstretched . . . And your home waters, your own island . . .'

Violet took two steps backward, she took two more, she turned away, her mouth bitter and her eyes burning. And just think, she told herself, giving the *sala* a sweeping glance and starting back down the length of it – just think, if in a few years' time by some crazy and happy-seeming chance in San Marcuola there's the wedding of his daughter and my son, there are scores of bedizened boats and delighted guests, afterward in this house there's feasting, music, dancing. Hugh and Valentina and I if we're still alive will tell one another how amused by this falling out of destinies Philip and Giacomo would have been – Hugh and I, though undoubtedly not Valentina, probably by midnight having drunk a bit much. And it won't mean Robbie and Gloria's marriage is particularly likely to make them happy, after the first year or two or three. No, they'll do better each to fall in love a good few more times, as they probably will, and to be happy and unhappy in ways – in ways – I'll never know much about in what ways.

XXIX

Earlier that morning, when it had been Gloria's turn to sit with her father upstairs, his eyes had been shut. Minutes had passed. She'd kept watch over his head in its Levantine fez, over his white face with its noble forehead and nose and its flabby lower part, over his chest with its infinitesimal rise and fall, as she had done so many times. And as she'd sat there, suddenly there'd been what felt like a spasm in her brain.

In panic and in despair she had been convinced that, because the prospect of his dying was so frightful, so far she'd only *thought* she'd grappled with what was about to occur, but she hadn't really. But Papa truly *was* going to leave her! He was going away for ever, she was going to lose his talk and his love, it was all over! Men were going to bury him! What would happen when she needed him in years to come and he wasn't there? Her lips had parted, her lungs had heaved, her throat had clogged. She'd gazed at him with her mouth trembling and rivulets of tears on her cheeks, trying not to gasp aloud or to snuffle so as not to wake him up.

Papa had opened his eyes. A faint frown of distress had appeared on his forehead, but then his smile had taken hold. 'Don't cry, Gloria,' he'd said, in his whisper. 'This dying is nothing.' And then, after a silence, still smiling: 'You'll be all right, my darling, and so will I.'

She had nodded, dumb, miserable, but also thankful. He had turned his head aside, to let her wipe her eyes and blow her nose without being looked at. But then she saw that he'd noticed something on the window or by the window; he was fixing whatever it was with his old wry curiosity.

She'd leaned forward and across him, steadying herself with a hand on the rattan arm-rest of his chair, she'd looked where he was looking. At a corner of the window, in a cobweb that neither Elena nor anyone else had got around to removing, a blow-fly had blundered into that clinging net, and the spider with its long reach had crawled out for it.

Papa had been watching that ghastly, hopeless fight. Now, realising that she was watching it with him, he'd turned his head back to her, his eyes glittering with amusement. Look, my darling! his eyes had said. Here we are, that poor old bluebottle and I, both caught in the toils of the same problem and both still struggling a little. But that's all it is. Don't be too upset.

Mamma had come in and had told her to hurry and put on her black dress and her black shoes and hat, it had been impossible to think. But later in the morning, when Gloria stood in the Madonna dell'Orto for the mass with Francesco on her left and her mother on her right, instead of her

238

thoughts helter-skeltering through her brain pell-mell as they often did, everything was slowed, everything was stilled.

It was cool in the great barn-like nave. While the ritual was being recited for the next hour, nothing would be required of her. She felt detached behind her veil; she decided she rather liked looking at things through these dark speckles. She didn't have to listen to the familiar Latin pronouncements and sing-song, let alone think about them. For this lapse of time, her spirit was free. She had incense in her nostrils, and a damp mustiness this church seemed to harbour even in summer, and a dash of sandalwood that she thought came from the lady standing next to Robbie's godfather, all three of which she liked. Her ideas came lapping into her mind, one after the other, like ripples on the sand.

There was how attached she was to her cousin Stefano and how guilty she felt when she thought of him up there at La Badia, where last summer they hadn't be able to go for their usual month because of how close the Front was, and this year they couldn't go because of Papa. (Even after the greatest Austrian advances south, La Badia had never been in enemy hands. But for months Italian troops had been bivouacked there, and a few long-range shells had fallen on the property, including one that demolished the dovecote.) Yes, honestly she'd been out of her wits to day-dream about taking Robbie Mancroft there! That would have to be for after Stefano fell in love with somebody else.

There was what a bore Mamma could be, with her endless anxiety to get Francesco and her what she called 'settled' in this disheartening way or in that uncalled-for way. She was a bore too with her hesitant but repeated lamentations that the two of them didn't confide in her as freely as they'd used to – and all this was especially irksome this summer, when the moment you formulated a resentful thought about poor Mamma you felt dreadful for having done so. And the fact of the matter was . . . (Gloria's gaze travelled lightly and meditatively beyond the soaring columns into the side-aisles, it found out tombs and paintings. This was as it had been ever since she could remember when at the top of the house she propped her elbows on the sill of her bedroom window, she mused, misty ideas began to cluster, began to lose their mistiness.) Well, Francesco and she had grown so old this year! – or so it seemed to her this minute, joining in the ordained responses with the rest of the congregation, but aware that she was doing so only from the tiny sensation of her lips parting and touching, parting and touching again. Certainly from this year onward it was going to be a matter of them looking after Mamma, not the other way around. Old, old, she felt sometimes! Now, for instance. As old as this church, as old as the Grand Canal, because— No, no, she interrupted herself, *don't* glance around. All the same, a few paces to one side and slightly behind her, Robbie was looking at her, she knew he was.

There was how Papa had understood her tears. Not for a second had he been exasperated. Instead he'd at once tried to give her some of his courage and his strength. He'd tried to help, to show her how best to tackle this, how to go forward through this. And she felt strengthened, as she stood here with this chanting in her ears, with these ideas in her stilled mind, and she knew who was giving her this strength.

As soon as she came out of the church, all Gloria's high spirits returned, no doubt in natural reaction to the morning she'd had. Instead of feeling horror at her father's approaching extinction, she couldn't wait to be arranging his lunch on his walnut tray and carrying it up to him. She forgot the young men whose names were inscribed on the war memorial. Not wishing to run the risk of ending up in the same gondola as Donatella, she declared that she was going to walk home. When Hugh Thurne said that he'd go on foot too, she put up her veil and set off beside him merrily, talking about the dance classes she'd been going to, and a very handsome schooner from Trieste that had sailed in the other evening and anchored off St Mark's, and how since her father had been ill she'd gone out first thing each morning on her own to buy the *brioches*.

The lunch party started late and went on for most of the afternoon, with long lulls between the courses. These turned out to be more numerous than anticipated, because first Gloria recollected that Hugh Thurne was a keen devourer of the finest cheeses that the dairies of the Venetian hinterland produced (he was not aware of having a reputation for particular voracity, but he acceded to this cheerfully), and half an hour later she decided that, just because no pudding had been concocted for the occasion, that didn't mean she shouldn't go to the larder and return bearing the *tiramisu* that had been scrumptious yesterday and a good half of which remained.

Gloria kept darting away from the dining-room to see her father for a few minutes, with the excuse of finding out if

241

she could tempt him with some cheese or some pudding – or with no excuse at all, simply standing up from the table and walking quickly off. When the sun at last was low enough for the awnings to be raised, she vanished away to the top storey to change into an old cotton dress that she often wore to go rowing (it was a checked dress, of soft blues and pinks and greys), because she was going to take Robbie back to his house in the *sandolo*.

The planks of the jetty were warm after the day's sun had beaten on them, and so was the planking of the family's two boats moored there. The evening was golden and brackish and soft.

Gloria skipped into the gondola, making it rock slightly, skipped out of it into her own skiff alongside, and began casting off the two warps fore and aft. 'You row,' she said to Robert. 'I'll be able to row as much as I want to on my way home again, after I've got rid of you.'

Robert had the disadvantage of still being dressed in the suit he had put on for the commemorative mass. But he took off his tie and stuffed it into his jacket pocket, he undid the top button of his shirt. Gloria seated herself on the thwart expectantly, looking up at him with her black eyes, so on an impulse he took off his jacket and without saying anything he flopped it across her knees for her to hold. Then he stooped, he fitted the carved walnut *forcola* into the starboard gunwale. He picked up his oar, got his feet into the right position so that his weight in the boat felt right. He nudged his oar into the bight of the *forcola* and began to swing it into action. Up and over, not back and forth, he reminded himself, trying to get into the effective rhythm with his oar right away and not fumble and splash and waver. Up and over, and then that feathering twist with the blade to steer . . .

Robert had other disadvantages too. Although Gloria and he had begun to be taught Venetian oarsmanship by Francesco together at Easter, all through May and June, when at Eton he'd been playing cricket, she'd been going out on the water most evenings and becoming adept. And not only was sculling a *sandolo* when you hadn't had all that many lessons or much practice difficult enough, especially when you were required to perform this miracle of adroitness while looking at a girl whose loveliness only a few feet before your eyes made consciousness of all else impossible; his tormentress had other advantages over him too. She knew Venice inside out, while he was still joyfully emerging from familiar vistas to unfamiliar ones, still often thinking he knew which facade they were idling past but then discovering to his chagrin that they were several canals from it. And although generally Gloria and he, when language was needed, got on splendidly in their mishmash of Italian, English and French, she had the habit, especially when he'd been floundering along not too disastrously in dog-Italian, of retreating into Venetian. What was more, as they set off onto the Grand Canal from her parents' watergate with him at the oar, they were both tinglingly aware of what lay ahead of them, when the skiff should be let drift to a standstill. Perhaps in a backwater, beneath a bridge. Perhaps where a fig tree (there was one near San Francesco della Vigna, there was another behind the Albrizzi) arched over a drowsy canal where no boats ever seemed to pass.

243

'Row me . . .' Gloria cocked her head on one side, her eyes glimmered. 'Row me to San Zan Degolà, please. What, can't you remember where that is? And then take me round behind San Giacomo dell'Orio to . . . Oh, I'll tell you as we go along, if you haven't toppled overboard by then.'

A couple of hours later, Gloria's mood had seesawed once more. She had put Robert ashore at Ca' Zante. She had taken off her espadrilles, because she liked to be barefoot when she stood at her oar. Dusk had come, the first lights were glowing over the water. She rowed away, happy to be on her own, toward the Accademia bridge, just giving a lazy push and slow twist to her oar once in a while to keep the slender hull gliding forward.

The sultry sea air on her face, on her throat, on her arms; the stars that before long would begin to appear (she glanced back east over her shoulder – yes, the evening star was already there); the sensual delight of being poised straight and still at her oar, poised with the lithe hull stirring beneath her soles on the water . . . For a minute Gloria wanted to stay afloat till midnight or for that matter till morning. She wanted to turn off into the narrow windings of the labyrinth, go sculling alone for hours past lanterns gleaming at the keystones of arches, her mind calm, expectant.

Then she remembered her father at his windows, his lamp lit now. He was waiting for her, of that she had no doubt. So she didn't turn off down a tenebrous cleft between the palaces either to the left or to the right. She kept rowing up the Grand Canal, but glad that it was the length it was, going very gently. In a while there'd be Ca' Balbi on her left, she thought, and after that Ca' Mocenigo on her right – and then it would still be a fair way to Rialto. Then after Rialto . . . All these bats swooping past her, vanishing skyward, flitting back again! And the gulls were not flying any more now that it was growing dark, they were greyish-white blobs on the water.

XXX

As for who I'm becoming or where I'm going. As for the whys and the wherefores of this wandering widow, and what my uses in this world may be, apart from my loving you ... Can I settle for just being your adoring mother, is that all right?

Robert had nearly been asleep, but now he was utterly awake. Beyond his bedroom, the lantern on the loggia was still shining above the round wicker table and the chairs where his mother and he had eaten their supper. So that was how it was, he thought, still hearing her voice ghostlily. The living could haunt you just as the dead did. They were the same, they were voices, they were stories.

He swung his feet out of the bed, he opened the French window and went out onto the loggia in his pyjamas. The night was hot, with a canopy of stars. Moths were flittering. He sat down on one of the chairs, making the wicker creak, his knees up and his arms hugging them, remembering the splatter of his oar when he'd made an awkward stroke this evening, remembering Gloria's dimples when he'd veered too close to a ruinous wall and she'd had to fend off. A wastepipe had dripped, there'd been a rat swimming ahead making grey chevrons on the water, there'd been an old woman on a balcony watering her pots of geraniums. Then for a moment against the blade of his oar a bloated, almost hairless carcass had bumped, a small dog or a big cat, but he was getting used to the foul things that bobbed in the canals.

'Let's tie up in the shade,' Gloria had said. It was always she who decided when the rowing should cease and the kissing should start. 'No, not here. Under the next bridge, where it's all shadowy. The backwaters of this city must have seen an awful lot of wonderful cuddling since the place was founded, wouldn't you say?'

Up in the loggia long after midnight, Robert rested his chin on his knees, his delighted eyes gazing away over the roofs. He wondered where his godfather had gone this evening, because for some reason he felt like talking to him. He remembered the bridge at San Boldo, and how he'd kneeled on the floorboards and drawn Gloria toward him, in that narrow band of lapping dimness beneath the grey arch. Well, he certainly couldn't talk to his godfather Hugh about how unbelievably soft Gloria was in her thin dress when he held her to him, what it felt like when his hands moved on her, what it felt like when he kissed her lips, Robert thought. And he smiled to himself, brushing a mosquito away from his neck, his mind tumbling with sensual impressions, with ideas, with the need to sift all these and see what endured.

Did he really want to talk to his godfather sooner or later

about some of his notions this summer? About the vast change, since his father died, between a rooted life in England and this wandering? About perhaps discovering things in Italy that he'd thought he'd lost? – or rather, discovering that rediscovery *could* happen, the past could come flooding back in happiness and not in pain.

Yes, he felt perhaps his godfather *would* be the right person. Certainly he couldn't bring to mind anybody else who'd think his musings made much sense. And they'd already begun to talk more than they'd used to, when it was just the two of them going to visit a church or going out to lunch. The last time they'd been at a restaurant together, having a terrific feast of clams followed by inkfish and polenta, he'd tried to explain a little bit about how responsible his mother and he each felt for the other, and how this could be a problem because it was bad luck on the other one if you were *too* anxious. Even more hesitantly, and in answer to some very gentle questioning, he'd explained that yes, he still seemed to talk to his father all the time and to hear his voice. In a strange sort of fashion, they were just as close in memory as they'd ever been in physical fact. Oh Lord, he'd said, he knew that he wasn't expressing it very brilliantly – but did Godfather Hugh understand? And the good thing was that gradually he was getting better at this remembering and imagining than he had been at first, it didn't always upset him so horribly as before. Things were settling down in his head – well, they had to, didn't they? The dreadful change had been made; he'd grappled with it, he was getting used to it.

All around Venice, how evenly the levels of light lay on

the lagoon! Last Saturday when Francesco had been free the
three of them had been out in the gondola from after breakfast till evening, wearing straw hats in the hope that the sun
wouldn't definitively addle their brains. They'd rowed away
to the north past Le Vignole to the island of Sant'Erasmo,
Francesco lording it on the stern deck, Gloria and he taking
turns at the other oar forward. And it had been just like on
the harbours and the meres of his old home, if you allowed
for a few local differences such as having egrets instead of
grebes. The coast he'd discovered and the coast where he'd
been a boy both had their shore woods, their church towers,
their creeks, their wide, wide skies.

England or Italy, before the war or after the war, in his
father's company or with his spirit beside him . . . He'd been
sad, remembering. But for those miraculous hours he'd also
been nearly – well, *what* had he been? Nearly victorious?
There'd been brackish hayfields whispering to the tide's
change, there'd been marshes of sea lavender. He'd breathed
woodsmoke, a curlew had cried. His eyes and his heart had
been at peace out on those tideways, because it had been just
like when Daddy and he had sailed *Calypso* on English estu-
aries, and this time the past had come echoing back as strength
and richness, the past and the present had chimed.

There'd been a day moon over shipping in a channel, a
breeze that ruffled a clump of willow trees, skeins of wildfowl
on the wing. Sad and happy, happy and sad, he'd seemed to
rediscover a rightness to himself that he'd thought was lost, a
rightness of the moment to the mind, or something like that
– and if these harmonies in his head were possible, if hours

such as this were going to visit him however rarely, there was hope. Oh, it was just a question of where you'd been a child, probably. Or it was something in your marrow-bone or in your blood. For heaven's sake, having Gloria in the boat beside him was probably all the explanation that was required.

Robert jumped to his feet, pulled on his red dressing-gown, knotted its belt in a voluminous bow, forgot his slippers, and set off down the staircase to find out if his godfather was still up, or anyway to have a wander through the house and enjoy his mind being so awake this late at night. Even if he did bump into his godfather, they'd probably end up talking about something quite different.

His bare feet liking the cool stone, he strayed beneath arches and pediments all over the second floor. A lot of lights were still lit, their effulgence shimmering on ornate picture frames, on wall hangings, on the marbles of fireplaces. Robert remembered stories of the Venetian past that he'd read or he'd been told, he imagined the merchant princes who'd had their splendours and their deaths here. His godfather had told him about a duchess who'd entertained her lovers in this house. And a famous cardinal had ended his life in one of these rooms, so he imagined the cowls and the candles as a pyx was carried to the death-bed. He imagined dancing with Gloria here hundreds of years ago, in Titian's time. A window in the music-room had been left open. A cockchafer flew in from the darkness, whirred slowly past the chandelier.

He went down another flight, and as he came into the drawing-room on that floor he heard the chink of glass. He saw Hugh Thurne's tall, black-clad figure stooping slightly

as he poured from a decanter. Then it did occur to Robert
that his entrance on bare feet must have been soundless, and
even that his appearance in his godfather's part of the house
in the middle of the night in his dressing-gown might seem
odd. But when he said, 'Hello, Godfather Hugh, I didn't
mean to startle you,' the response was only a trifle surprised.

'Oh hello, dear lad.' Thurne raised his whisky glass, he
sipped. 'You haven't had a bad dream, or anything like that,
have you? They can be horrible, dreams.'

'No. Not at all. I was . . . It's an amazing night, have you
seen the stars? I was wide awake, so I sat in the loggia for a
bit, and then I . . . Well, I seem to have just come wandering.'

Thurne took his gold watch out of his waistcoat pocket,
looked at it, put it back. 'We'd better not stay up *much* later
or we'll find ourselves listening to the dawn chorus and then
we'll want to go on listening to it. We'll lean out of the
windows to watch for the first hint of daybreak, or we'll go
down and sit in the garden, and one way or another we'll be
done for. I know what I'm like, I've wasted my time in those
sorts of delectable ways far too often. But since you're here
. . . I've just got back from a party, that's why I'm still on my
legs, and like you I didn't feel like going to sleep.' He gestured
hospitably toward various chairs. 'You're not thirsty, hungry?
I mustn't offer you a shot of this merciful stuff, I'm afraid.
But would you like a glass of wine?'

'Thank you.' Robert watched the dark red rise half-way
up the glass.

'Now, dear lad, tell me about . . . oh, happy things . . .
about anything you fancy.'

XXXI

Giacomo Venier had been exhausted by the mental effort that he had expended in his conversation with Hugh Thurne. Then an hour later he'd been more debilitated by his attempts to respond to his wife and his daughter than he'd been forti- fied by his fillet of bass, his slice of bread and his glass of white wine. He had drifted into a half-sleep.

For months, his life had been this alternation: he would come up into a weary awakeness, he would sink down into a miasma where muddled, depressing impressions or dreams followed each other. But this was different. The pain in his head was worse, but he couldn't reach out for the handbell on the table beside him. If he could only ring it, Valentina would come. She would give him some more from that phial with the stopper. He would go down, down, there'd be less of this. Once more he tried to see the table, he tried to make a move toward the bell or toward the phial, but nothing happened.

He must have had another stroke – yes, he thought, muzzy

and frightened, probably that was it. He couldn't remember when any blood to speak of had last drubbed in his heart, but it was beating in his head. Hurt, hurt, hurt, it went.

Perhaps she was here already, perhaps she'd been here all the time. He still didn't seem able to see anything. She . . . Valentina or Gloria. If he could say something, she would lean over him. Old Zanon would arrive, he'd hold his wrist to feel if anything much was still going on, he'd disappear.

They hadn't yet helped him to bed, he wasn't flat on his back, he could sense that. So he was still in his chair, it couldn't be all that late. Strange, for how long this had been gestating within him, for how long today had been waiting for him. Ever since that indecipherable early version of him, that forbidding harbinger, had nestled in his mother's womb.

Then he had come up to the surface, because he could see the shadowy *sala* where he was lying back in his chair, he could see that night was falling and that his brass lamp had been lit (he even scented its oily wick), and he saw Valentina, who was leaving the room. In the distance by the door she turned to look back at him. For a moment he wanted to speak (he was sure that he could have done that now, though before it would have been impossible). In a flicker of time he imagined how she would be pleased, she would walk back past the sofas and the drum table toward him. He would whisper, 'Darling, I feel awful. I think I may have had another stroke.' She would say something like, 'Yes, my love, I'm afraid you may have done. I was just going to send for Dr Zanon, it won't take me a minute. But here I am. I'll stay here with you. Much better.'

But Giacomo didn't say a word. Now that he was perfectly conscious, the sense of his own failure had suffused his spirit so vilely that it would have been unbearable to be with anyone. Valentina went out, he was alone. He gazed around. This room where his brother and he had romped when they were children, the whole house, which year after year he had loved and which, he now realised, had been the incarnation of any meagre significance his life had possessed, aroused in him no emotion whatsoever except for a cold weariness.

At no season of his life, when he was thirty, when he was twenty, for that matter even when he was ten, had he been consumed with any particular ambition, or even been propelled by anything that you could decently call a passion, he thought bitterly. So what had he ever amounted to? He'd practised a profession, and at work and in society he'd hoped for the respect of those he respected. He'd taken an interest in his city's past and in its present – but he knew how futile that had been. He'd tried to make a little money. He'd sat on the governing bodies of the Fenice theatre, of the Marciana library, of the Red Cross in this neck of the north-east Italian woods . . . But none of these was an achievement. His profession hadn't even been a wish, merely a need, and he hadn't fulfilled it well.

He'd dedicated himself to his wife and children, as everyone said. But the care and love of your family were something that an inspired man did when he had time and heart left over, and he had never been inspired, and now he was abandoning Valentina and the children when possibly a bit of help and cherishing might have been useful to them. (He saw this coldly, staring at the pale column by his right hand, at the shadowy Grand Canal beyond and below.) And anyhow, the cherishing of your wife and children was something for the biologists to explain, not the poets; it was a mist, he'd soon be through it. The cruel thing was that he'd never know what became of them, and the foolish thing was that he minded. Francesco, who at twenty was young to be the man of the family, but not so young as all that; Francesco who was learning to work doggedly and, when the initial perturbation of his own death this year had been made suitably little of, would go on putting his back into it because he'd want the rewards of that. He'd take up his regattas again before long, which would unquestionably be a good thing. In the evenings after he'd worked hard he'd go out to his friends and his dinners and his amusements, he'd play hard too and good luck to him. Gloria . . .

His lamp wasn't the only light. Outside the windows in the gloaming there was a ring around the moon, and he remembered seeing Gloria set off in her little boat – when? a few hours ago? – to take his godson back to his other godfather's house. If he watched, perhaps he'd see her rowing home up the reach toward him.

In a lull between two crescendos of the blood-beat in his head, Giacomo thought he heard his own voice say: 'Really, darling, don't you think you ought to take a lantern when you go rowing after dark?' He heard her answer: 'Oh no, Papa, I like it like this.'

A ring around the moon, the Grand Canal like dark glass, and Gloria coming for him in that scruffy old skiff she liked . . . So that was it! They were all going to sally forth on the water after dinner, just like in the happiest times. Valentina and Francesco must be here too, only he couldn't see them.

His brain had never been so easy to hurt. It was being touched again, lightly but all the time, and then ever less lightly. It was being hit by blood, by pain. Then the beating faded away. He was at the water-gate in the moonlight, leaning on his stick. Gloria was standing in her boat, one hand on a mooring post, the other hand on her oar, meeting him with her eyes.

'You see, here I am,' she seemed to say. 'Shall we go, you and I?'

Here came the pain once more. Gloria was blurred, he lost her. Then the mooring in the moonlight was there again. Water lapping. Her waiting eyes.

XXXII

'Well, he played the hand of cards he'd been dealt, and you can't ask more of a fellow than that. Say what you like, he was one of the last of an old school. And I don't suppose that now . . .'

'Oh I don't know, why do you say that? Francesco seems to me to be a fine young man. Got rather more fire in him than his father had, if anything.'

'Sold? You mean the house? Is that what people are saying? Oh Lord, I do hope not! If their situation is really that bad, couldn't they let a floor to visitors, or something like that? And in an old place that big, surely it ought to be possible to make a couple of flats in the back somewhere.'

In front of the house that had belonged to Giacomo Venier, in the late afternoon the Grand Canal had filled with Venetian craft of every kind. From gunwale to gunwale, conversations eddied. It seemed that everybody who had known Venier (and he had been acquainted with half Venice) was waiting for his coffin to be carried downstairs to the water-gate, loaded aboard a gondola for its final journey through the maze of the city and then out into the lagoon to the graveyard island.

Women used their fans. Men lifting their hats courteously in greeting took the opportunity to pat their foreheads with their handkerchiefs. Already the Grand Canal between the Venier house and the church of San Stae opposite was so clogged that it was impossible to row into the dense mass of drifting hulls, so the last boats to arrive came to a standstill fifty yards or more to the east or the west where there was still a little free water to manoeuvre in. The steersmen used their oars sufficiently to keep the scores of craft from bumping into one another, but apart from that stood idle. Families gave up trying to come alongside particular friends of theirs, they chatted to whoever happened to be next to them.

'By the way, have you seen Gloria recently? This year she's grown into an absolute stunner. Take a good look at her when they appear at the gate, before she gets into a boat and sits down. Yes, yes, dreadfully immoral thoughts for an occasion like this, I know – how boring do you reckon to be? But when she's cheered up a bit, I'm going to enjoy it the next time I bump into her at a party.'

'He wasn't old, he just looked old. Well, he's off to lie beside his mother and father.'

'Say what you like, one minute you've got your legs under your own dining-table, your family are all around you and maybe an old friend has dropped by as well, there's a decent dinner, there's a bottle of wine. Then the next thing is, you're in a wooden box and they're carting you out of your front door feet first. Oh look, here they come. We'll be on our way soon.'

Seated in the Ca' Zante boat beside Hugh Thurne, with Robert on the diminutive chair in the bows, Violet Mancroft remembered the spring night when she'd been rowed back here up the Grand Canal. She remembered half seeing all the dances that had been held behind the windows in these palace facades for hundreds and hundreds of years; she remembered half hearing the music. For a moment, in the fleet of motionless boats waiting in the sunlight, she was transfixed by a music that had quivered into silence long ago and yet still was in the air – a music that was grave but defiant, self-knowing, amused, already dying away again.

Then she saw Francesco Venier and his cousin Stefano Moretta, with their hats in their hands, come out of the canal gate and stand respectfully one to each side, plainly aware of the great concourse of vessels there before them to render homage to the dead man, but not paying attention to that. The chatter in the boats was hushed. The bearers came out with the coffin, Valentina and Gloria following them. And Violet with a single pulse of her heart *was* Valentina. She knew how Valentina was holding herself together to perform this last rite in a manner that was dignified and worthy of Giacomo and of herself. She knew that she would succeed immaculately (she also knew that Valentina herself knew that she would succeed), all through the slow procession of black boats out to San Michele, through the funeral service, the burial, the coming home, the talk, the solicitude. She knew, too, the corrosive processes that would start to operate within her friend tonight after her years' task and love were done, processes partly recognised and partly denied, which

261

would be irresistible when she was alone in the house with her son and her daughter, and which would go on, when she was more alone.

The first gondola to set off eastward down the Grand Canal, all the other vessels making way for it, was rowed fore and aft by two men in black breeches and black tunics, and bore Giacomo Venier in his coffin amidships. Immediately astern it was followed by his own boat, rowed by a hired gondolier (Francesco had been obliged to submit to this), bearing the widow and her children. After them, the fleet began sluggishly to move off down the windless channel into the hush, into the pinks and the golds and the blues, those who were related to the principal actors or who were particularly long-established friends keeping to the front of the procession, others feeling more at their ease and less constrained by gloom thirty or fifty boats back. The pious crossed themselves, and recollected primly that Venier had not asked for a priest when he was dying, nor had his wife sent for one. Gondoliers flicked their cigarettes into the water. A child's laughing voice rang out and was suppressed.

'Which way are we going?'

'What do you mean, which way are we going? There's only one way that old Giacomo Venier can go, so far as I'm aware. Oh, I see what you mean. Up past the Santi Apostoli, that'll be the canal they take.'

'What sort of fellow was he, really, I wonder? I mean – apart from the not very much that he ever got around to actually doing in his life. But . . . to himself, how was he, who was he, do you suppose?'

'Do you know, it's an odd thing, but . . . I was at their wedding and . . . Well, Valentina when she was twenty-two was quite pretty. Of course, then before their first child was born they had . . . Well, she wasn't always lucky with her pregnancies. She had a horrible few years.'

As she sat beside her mother, Gloria's entire soul was gripped onto the fact that her father had bequeathed her this city to know as he had known it and to love as he had loved it, he'd left her this tattered glory, and she was going to be true to that. This was the way in which she was going to honour him, always – so to begin with as the cortège set off she kept thinking this, in order not to cry. She was determined not to cry again until she was in her bedroom tonight, but her throat was still aching with tears, so nervously she started to make herself notice things that couldn't possibly cause anyone to whimper and gasp and sob. As they came past the Santi Apostoli the bell was ringing, so she listened attentively to that. She made herself focus on the faces of the passers-by who stopped at their approach, who took off their hats and crossed themselves. She looked at a broken watergate that was off its hinges, at her own hand on the gunwale where the paint was cracked.

They were leaving the city now. The long file of vessels, released from the narrow enfilades of brick and peeling plaster, of balconies and windows, began to spread out. From a few boats behind Gloria, Robert saw San Michele with its cypresses ahead. Beyond lay all the northern lagoon, with its channels and fishing villages, its shoals where the white egret waded. But the promise of wide skies and the promise of islands

263

reminded Robert that next month he'd be in England, he'd be at university, in a life in which Gloria would have no part at all. He twisted uneasily in his seat.

Hugh Thurne had remembered the last time he'd talked to Giacomo Venier, only a couple of days ago. The dying man had asked him about how the last details of the various peace treaties were being thrashed out, about how all that was going, so he'd told him. Giacomo had listened. Then he'd replied in his whisper that the whole thing would depend on whether the British-French alliance held steady, whether for a good few decades yet they kept Germany weak enough not to be a problem or they flinched from that, whether they kept the Rhineland demilitarised or they didn't, whether they kept Germany and Austria from ganging up together again. Because if not, well, you couldn't be precise about how old Francesco and Robert and Gloria would be when it occurred – but they'd have to live through another European war unless he was much mistaken. Or rather, they'd find themselves attempting to live through another war, and attempting to bring through it any children they might have had.

That had been while the armada of boats was still moving slowly east down the Grand Canal. Then Hugh's thoughts had zigzagged. He'd recalled Robert in his dressing-gown in the middle of the night in the drawing-room, Robert being really very sensible about his father's death, not deluding himself that you could ever put such a thing utterly behind you or not be haunted by it, but saying that he'd grappled with it, he was getting used to living with it, which was the best you could expect. He'd thought of how, now that Gloria, too, had lost her father, those two were going to have more romantic muddled-upness to bind them together not less, and he'd wondered whether this promised well or it didn't. He'd been aware of Violet sitting beside him, how rakishly beautiful she was in black.

And here he was, the only survivor of a trio of friends and the least deserving of the three, it went without saying – here he was, bobbing about on the water in the midst of this fleet of other boats, on his way to San Michele where the bone-white facade was catching the evening sun. Here he was, certainly not an inch farther advanced in any intelligent direction than he'd been the year before, with the same longing to distrust his self-knowledge and the same longing to trust his hopes. And he still seemed to have his old readiness to think that maybe this time the intermittent flickering up of – of – oh Lord, of some inspiration or other – wasn't an *ignis fatuus*, wasn't only phosphorescence trembling into brief seductiveness somewhere out there in the marshes on a summer night.

Idolatry – when had it been that he'd realised that this was his lasting bedevilment? Forever being distracted and decoyed . . . Well, possibly false gods were all there were.

For an instant, while ahead of him Giacomo Venier was arriving at the church where he would be unshipped for the last time, Hugh saw this lagoon as it must have appeared a millennium and a half ago to the first fugitives from a breaking empire who had retreated here to build themselves a precarious, ignoble sanctuary on these mudbanks. These islands before him, some of which still had their shabby churches and houses, some of which were ruins encumbered by scraggy trees and by nettle-beds, some of which had subsided again beneath the dirty water so that only local historians, such as Giacomo had been, knew where once they'd had their monasteries or their villages, their quays, their tanned lateen sails swinging slack at the gaffs . . . He saw these places as they must have appeared in the beginning: unprepossessing reedbeds and shallows, useful as it turned out, offering hope.

The coffin had been lifted onto the bier, it was being trundled into the church. The first boats in the procession were being brought alongside the stone steps by their oarsmen so that the mourners could go ashore.

Unable to resist it, Hugh turned to Violet. For an instant he met the glimmer in her eyes. Then he stood up, ostensibly in order to offer her his arm when she should wish to disembark, but in fact to look out once more over the lagoon.